"So, you're training Callie to be Gammy's eyes?"

Jake nodded. "Myrna could live independently for years to come." Maintaining Myrna's independence was Jake's goal.

"What if I take over as Callie's Puppy Raiser? Then she could get used to living with Gammy."

Jake hadn't expected this. "Do you like dogs? I don't require my foster parents to have experience training, but they must have a love for dogs."

"Who doesn't love puppies?" Olivia smiled. "I've taken a sabbatical from my job with no set return date, so I can stay as long as it takes to get Callie trained. By then, I'll be able to better assess whether it's in my grandmother's best interest to stay in Bluebell or move to Miami and live with me."

Didn't Myrna get a say in the matter? Of course, that was between Olivia and her grandmother. "Okay then." He extended his hand. "It's a deal. We'll work together to get Callie trained if you agree to hold off on any decision about moving Myrna."

Weekdays, **Jill Weatherholt** works for the City of Charlotte. On the weekend, she writes contemporary stories about love, faith and forgiveness. Raised in the suburbs of Washington, DC, she now resides in North Carolina. She holds a degree in psychology from George Mason University and a paralegal studies certification from Duke University. She shares her life with her real-life hero and number one supporter. Jill loves connecting with readers at jillweatherholt.com.

Books by Jill Weatherholt

Love Inspired

Second Chance Romance
A Father for Bella
A Mother for His Twins
A Home for Her Daughter
A Dream of Family
Searching for Home
Their Inseparable Bond

Visit the Author Profile page at LoveInspired.com.

Their Inseparable Bond

Jill Weatherholt

LOVE INSPIRED

INSPIRATIONAL ROMANCE

LOVE INSPIRED®
INSPIRATIONAL ROMANCE

ISBN-13: 978-1-335-59860-8

PLEASE RECYCLE
THIS PRODUCT IS RECYCLABLE

Recycling programs
for this product may
not exist in your area.

Their Inseparable Bond

Love Inspired
22 Adelaide St. West, 41st Floor
Toronto, Ontario M5H 4E3, Canada
www.LoveInspired.com

Printed in U.S.A.

But Jesus beheld them, and said unto them,
With men this is impossible;
but with God all things are possible.
—*Matthew* 19:26

For Derek.
Thank you for your enduring patience
during my perpetual meltdowns.

Chapter One

Canine trainer Jake Beckett peered at his twins in the rearview mirror. Being a single father at the age of fifty had never been part of the plan. Then again, neither had losing his wife and their unborn child.

"Do you think Miss Myrna will bake her yummy snickerdoodle cookies for the class picnic?" Six-year-old Kyle called out from the back seat of Jake's cherry-red extended-cab pickup truck.

Myrna Hart's cookies were famous in the small town of Bluebell Canyon, Colorado. Without Myrna, the most beloved resident in town, Jake would have never survived that first year after his wife passed away.

"I don't see why not, but you can ask her yourself when we get to her house."

Jake stole a glance at his son. With his dark

brown eyes and sun-kissed brown hair, Kyle was the spitting image of his late mother. His twin sister, Kayla, had many of his wife's features, like her thick, wavy brown hair and rust-colored freckles that dotted the bridge of her nose, but Kyle favored their mother more.

Jake brought the vehicle to a stop at the intersection. Cumulus clouds drifted over the Rocky Mountains. He glanced over his shoulder and noticed Kayla gazing out the window, lost in thought. "Are you okay, Kayla? You haven't said a word since we left the school."

"She's upset about the mother-daughter fashion show." Kyle nudged his sister's arm.

"Stop it." Kayla pushed back and stuck out her tongue.

The family dog, Tank, a three-year-old Border collie nestled between the children, raised his head and released a snort.

"Settle down, kids. What's this about a fashion show, Kayla?"

The sudden silence was ominous. As time passed, Jake was coming to realize that as Kayla got older, not having a mother would bring challenges he might not be prepared to handle.

"Nothing... It's stupid." She choked back tears.

"Yeah, who cares about seeing a bunch of girls walking around wearing different clothes?"

Kyle said. "It's silly, Kay. Forget about it. We can go fishing or something instead."

Jake was proud of his son. Kyle always tried to protect his sister. It was best to drop the subject for now. The event obviously upset her.

Moments later, Jake pulled into the circular driveway in front of Myrna's house. Rocking chairs lined the large wraparound porch, tempting a person to settle down with a glass of icy lemonade. For the past two years, Myrna's door was always open. After Laura died while giving birth to what would have been their third child, Myrna's home had become a refuge for Jake and his children.

Jake raked a hand through his cropped salt-and-pepper hair, unbuckled his seat belt and opened the cab door. Tank sprang from the truck.

"I'll race you!" Kyle called out to his sister before sprinting toward the front porch.

Kayla zipped off with Tank on her heels.

The children thundered up the steps, ran across the wide-plank flooring and jerked open the squeaky screen door. Myrna had told them long ago they didn't need to call ahead or knock—they were family.

Jake's long, muscular legs circled to the rear of the truck to retrieve the replacement stairway railing. Myrna's diagnosis of macular degeneration had propelled him on a mission to make her house more accommodating and safer. Jake and others in the community looked after Myrna following the death of her husband, Jeb, five years ago.

He walked across the driveway carrying the railing and ascended the stairs. Tank circled the porch twice, exploring the wood with his wet nose. Then he headed to the oversize dog bed Myrna had bought specially for him.

"Lie down, Tank."

The dog spun around three times before flopping on the pillow and releasing a sigh.

"Good boy." Jake opened the door and stepped into the foyer. The toe of his leather work boot caught on the runner that covered the hardwood floor. Jake made a mental note to inspect the entire house for throw rugs. They were a tripping hazard. To ensure Myrna's safety, they would have to go.

Voices echoed from the kitchen. Jake moved past the baby grand piano to the back of the house. He inhaled the aroma of sweet cinnamon. He stepped inside the kitchen and Myrna's face brightened. Measuring in at barely five feet tall, Myrna kept fit by her constant motion. Her seventy-year-old skin showed no sign of the hours she spent outdoors in her garden.

"Jake, I just told the children your timing is

perfect. Not only are there fresh snickerdoodles, but you finally get to meet my beautiful grand-daughter and brilliant doctor, Olivia." Myrna winked and ran a finger through her short silver hair. "She flew into town last night for an overdue visit. It was a delightful surprise."

Jake's pulse ticked up when he spotted a striking young woman sitting on one of the stools surrounding the granite-topped island in the kitchen. Kyle was chatting up a storm with her like she was an old friend. Olivia's auburn, wavy hair cascaded over the tops of her shoulders.

Jake placed the railing against the laundry room door. He approached Olivia and extended his hand. He swallowed hard against the knot in his throat. "I've heard a lot about you. It's nice to meet you in person. I'm Jake Beckett."

Olivia smiled. She stood, revealing her long limbs and slender stature, and accepted Jake's hand. "Hello. Olivia Hart. It's a pleasure to meet you."

According to Myrna, Olivia worked long hours as an ER doctor in Miami, Florida. She was married, but he didn't remember Myrna ever mentioning children. Jake released her hand. At six foot one, it wasn't often he met a lady almost equal in height. "I didn't mean to interrupt your reunion. I thought I'd stop by and install the railing. I picked it up at the hardware store this morning since I'll be taking the kids to the car show tomorrow."

Myrna set the pitcher of sweet tea on the counter, then removed glasses from the cabinet. She glanced in her granddaughter's direction. "He has a mile-long list of improvements he'd like to make on the house. Jake is the most thoughtful young man you'll ever meet. He's always doing for others."

Jake's face warmed. "I'm not exactly young, but that's kind of you to say. I've added something to the list. We need to get rid of that runner in the foyer, along with the other throw rugs. They're a hazard."

"See, Gammy? Jake agrees with me. It's not safe for you to be living alone." Olivia addressed Myrna with a pointed look.

Jake shook his head. "I wouldn't say that. With some improvements and the help of a service dog, I think your grandmother will be fine."

"You're getting a dog?" Olivia glanced at her grandmother.

"Yes, and she's just the sweetest thing. Her name is Callie. Jake is training her." Myrna smiled and took a seat at the island.

Jake removed his wallet from his back pocket. He pulled out a business card and passed it to

Olivia. "My brothers and I run a business together. They're out of town on a hunting trip, otherwise they'd be here devouring your grandmother's cookies."

Olivia examined the card. "Beckett's Canine Training. So you train service dogs?"

He nodded and straightened his shoulders. "Yes, ma'am, along with herding dogs. We train and place service dogs across the state. I also host a camp four times a year for Puppy Raisers."

"Why don't you bring Callie with you for Sunday dinner so Olivia can get to know her?" Myrna suggested to Jake.

He'd thought about bringing Callie along today, but she wasn't behaving well this morning. Jake left her at his brother's house. Callie had proved to be a slow learner. She would never make it as an official service dog, but Jake was confident she could meet Myrna's needs if her vision deteriorated. "I'll do that." He grabbed two glasses Myrna had left next to the pitcher. "Do you want some tea, kids?"

"Yes, yes!" Kyle bounced on his toes.

Kayla remained silent while sneaking looks at Olivia.

"Kayla, what about you?"

"I'm not thirsty," she whispered.

"Don't forget the cookies." Myrna pointed to

the large porcelain Cheshire cat. "I had forgotten all about the car show tomorrow."

"We haven't," Kyle chirped. "Daddy said we could even stay until dark to watch the fireworks. It'll be so cool!"

Myrna looked at Jake. "Maybe you can take Olivia. I want her to experience everything that small-town life offers."

Olivia released a sigh and addressed Jake. "She's trying to convince me to give up my job and uproot my life in Miami." Olivia rolled her eyes. "Small-town life isn't for me."

"So, quaint and hospitable isn't your thing?" He laughed.

"I don't mean to be disrespectful. It's fine for some people." She drew her shoulders back.

"If you stick around long enough, you might change your mind." Jake couldn't imagine living anywhere else. He'd enjoyed growing up in Virginia, but after he and his brothers inherited the land in Bluebell nearly twenty years ago from their aunt who passed, the entire family had moved out West.

Olivia trailed her finger along the top of her glass of sweet tea. "I don't see that happening. But I will stay long enough to convince my grandmother to move back to Miami with me. So, the safety improvements and the dog training probably aren't necessary."

Jake's mouth dropped open. Wait. What? Was she serious? There was no way Jake could allow that to happen. Sure, he wasn't blood, but Myrna was family to him and his children.

Kyle moved closer to his father. Anguish filled his eyes. "Is Miss Myrna moving?"

Myrna sprang from her stool with the agility of a teenager. She opened the oak cabinet, removed a serving platter and scooped the cookies from the jar. Carefully, she placed them in a semicircle on the dish. "I'm not going anywhere. My home is here. It's where I plan to stay until I go home to be with the Lord." Myrna hurried to the island with the baked goods. "Let's change the subject and enjoy these cookies."

Kayla gave Olivia a callous once-over. After losing her mother, Kayla clung to Myrna. Two years had passed and their bond was stronger than ever. Kyle loved the older woman too, but Kayla and Myrna had a special connection that the little girl wasn't about to allow this interloper to destroy.

"Now, about the car show. You should go with Jake and the kids, Olivia." Myrna sat, broke off a piece of cookie and popped it into her mouth. "I think you'd have a good time. I won't be able to take you since I'll be baking cupcakes tomorrow morning and preparing for Bible study."

Jake considered Myrna's suggestion. It might

be a good idea for Olivia to go to the show. She'd hear firsthand how much the people in the community loved her grandmother. There wasn't a person in Bluebell who wouldn't help Myrna in a time of need. Maybe then Olivia would drop this outlandish idea to move her. "If you're interested, you're welcome to join the kids and me," Jake offered.

"Yes!" Kyle jumped off his stool and circled to Olivia. "Please come with us, Dr. Olivia. It'll be so much fun. We're going to have a picnic. Daddy's going to make us his special triple-decker club sandwiches. We even get to have soda, too!"

Olivia looked at Jake. Her brow arched. "What about your wife? Shouldn't you check with her?"

Silence covered the room like mist drifting across a pond.

Jake's stomach twisted. His eyes darted between the twins. Kayla's face turned to stone. Kyle's lower lip quivered.

"Our mommy is dead." Kayla's abrupt response shattered the silence.

Kyle ran to Jake and buried his face in his father's hip.

Embarrassed, Jake addressed his daughter. "Kayla, I think you should apologize to Dr. Olivia."

Kayla eyed her father. "It's true. I don't have a mommy anymore."

"That may be, but I didn't like your tone."

The adults exchanged glances. Kayla remained silent, crossed her arms and rolled her lower lip.

Olivia cleared her throat. "I'm so sorry." Olivia turned to her grandmother. "I guess I didn't remember."

The refrigerator's motor hummed. Outside, a car door slammed, and Tank barked twice.

"It sounds like I have more company." Myrna clapped her hands and rose from her seat. "So it's settled. Jake, you and the kids can swing by tomorrow morning and pick up Olivia on your way to the car show. I'll have a batch of cupcakes ready for the picnic."

Jake nodded. There was no point in arguing with Myrna.

Myrna headed to the door. Kayla remained quiet, and Olivia kept her eyes glued to the floor. Kyle inched toward Olivia's stool. "So, you'll go with us to the car show?"

"That's sweet of you, Kyle, but your father might want to keep this a family outing." Olivia looked up at Jake as though asking for permission.

"We would be happy for you to join us," Jake said.

"Please, will you come?" Kyle asked.

Olivia turned her attention back to Kyle and

smiled. "I've always loved triple-decker sandwiches. Of course I'll go."

Kyle pumped his fist and whispered a *yes*, perhaps not wanting to upset his sister, but it was too late. Kayla frowned at Jake before racing out the kitchen door and into the backyard to take refuge in the tree house. After his wife died, Jake had built the house for the kids on Myrna's property since the family spent so much of their time with Myrna.

"Please come and have some tea and cookies, Larry." Myrna returned to the kitchen with her guest.

For as long as Jake could remember, Larry Walker had been the branch manager of the only bank in town. He sometimes overlooked late payments when someone in the community experienced tough times. Larry was a good man. Jake extended his hand. "It's nice to see you. What brings you out this way?"

Larry placed his briefcase on the island and reached inside. "I need a couple of signatures from Myrna."

"For the home improvements. Don't you remember?" Myrna directed her question at Jake. "I took out a home equity line of credit to cover the cost. I know I mentioned it to you."

"You did. But I told you a loan wasn't necessary. I can do all the work for you."

Myrna smiled. "That's generous of you, but I can't let you work for free. Besides, I have to pay for the materials."

Jake wouldn't be working for free. He couldn't count the number of meals and counseling sessions Myrna had provided him since his wife died. He'd never be able to repay her in his lifetime. "You can pay for the material, but I won't accept a dime from you for the labor."

Myrna rolled her eyes and looked down at the papers Larry had placed in front of her. "Where do I sign?"

Larry flipped the pages and pointed to the signature block at the bottom of page three. "Right here."

Myrna blinked her eyes before rubbing her fingers over her eyelids.

"Where? Let me put on my reading glasses." Myrna removed the eyewear from the top of her head and slid them on her face.

The three adults watched as Myrna squinted to see the signature line. Her glasses didn't appear to help.

"Gammy, when was the last time you saw the eye doctor?" Olivia moved closer.

"I had a follow-up appointment a month ago, but I had to cancel."

"Why?" Olivia asked.

"Elizabeth from my prayer group needed a ride to Denver for her cataract surgery."

Myrna always put others ahead of herself.

Olivia shook her head. "This is exactly why you should come to Miami. It's not safe for you to drive a car if you can't see to sign your name. I can't allow you to put yourself in danger. You have macular degeneration. If you don't stay on top of this disease, you could lose your eyesight."

Jake agreed about the seriousness of Myrna's condition. Since her diagnosis, he'd researched the disease. He was aware of what could happen if Myrna didn't receive proper treatment. Jake had found a well-regarded specialist in Denver and put Myrna's name on the waiting list for an appointment. But if Olivia had her way, Myrna would never have that appointment. Jake couldn't allow that to happen. Completing the safety improvements on Myrna's home and training Callie would be his top priorities. Jake had every intention of proving to Olivia that Myrna belonged in Bluebell, surrounded by the people who loved her.

"Good morning, sleepyhead." Myrna stood at the six-burner gas stove. A white-and-yellow apron hugged her waist.

A heavy sensation filled Olivia's chest. Her

father used to call her "sleepyhead." Olivia often reflected on how different her life would have been if her father hadn't died when she was young. Her bare feet padded across the pine-wood floor leading to her grandmother's kitchen. "Good morning." She hugged the woman and held on a little longer than usual. The tension she hadn't known she'd been carrying eased. "It's nice to be here with you, Gammy. I've missed you."

Myrna smiled. "I've missed you, too."

"I'm sorry I let so much time pass."

"There's no need to apologize. I still carry fond memories of the cruise you took me on several years ago. And remember, you visited a couple times when you attended medical conferences in Denver."

"Those were brief evening visits before I had to get back to Miami." Olivia lowered her gaze. "I should have spent more time with you."

"You're a busy doctor. And with the divorce, I'm sure it's been difficult. I only wish you would have told me about your marital issues before you arrived in Bluebell. Maybe I could have helped you."

Olivia hadn't shared the details of the breakup with Gammy or anyone. She'd been in shock when her ex-husband told her he no longer wanted to have children. Her world went into a tailspin when Mark filed for divorce. Olivia wanted to work on their differences, but Mark believed it was best to end the marriage since he no longer shared her dream of having a family. "I'm not sure anyone could have helped, but there's no excuse for me not to have called you more frequently."

"You're here now. That's what's important. Breakfast is almost ready. I'm sure you're starving."

The aroma of bacon with a hint of sweetness caused her stomach to rumble. "I am. Why didn't you wake me up last night?" Olivia headed to the coffeepot. She removed a cup from the mug tree and poured. A baking sheet lined with a dozen cupcakes cooled on the countertop.

"After Liz dropped me off from my caring cards meeting, you were sleeping so sound, I didn't have the heart." Myrna speared a strip of bacon with a fork and turned it over. She reduced the flame. Hot grease hissed inside the skillet.

Olivia couldn't remember when she'd slept so soundly. During the separation and following the divorce, with no one waiting for her at home, Olivia often covered for her colleagues who had families. "I don't think I've slept that long since I was in high school." She laughed and took a sip of the hot brew.

Myrna slid four slices of whole wheat bread into the toaster. "Between the time difference and the stress of traveling, you needed your rest. Since you slept through dinner, I've cooked you a big breakfast."

"That's so thoughtful. Thank you." Olivia took notice of the farmhouse table with five place settings. "Are you expecting company?"

"Since Jake was so sweet with his offer to take you to the car show today, I thought inviting him and the children over for breakfast was the least I could do." Myrna removed the second batch of cupcakes from the oven.

"Here, let me help you." Olivia grabbed a pot holder from the counter and took the baked goods from her grandmother. "It's only nine o'clock. I can't believe how much cooking and baking you've done. Do you ever slow down?"

"I could ask you the same. I worry about you working such long hours at the hospital." Myrna opened the refrigerator and removed a plate of cupcakes.

Olivia wanted to cut back her hours now, but when her marriage was crumbling, she'd used her job to escape the truth. The man she'd vowed to spend the rest of her life with had decided he no longer wanted to have children. "If you move to Miami, we can look after each other. I can reduce my hours. Or maybe I can leave the hospital and start a small family practice of my own that could offer more flexibility." Olivia bit her lower lip. "What if something happened to you? You're all alone in this big house."

Myrna placed the dessert on the counter and rested her hand on Olivia's arm. "You're thinking about your father, aren't you?"

Since Olivia had learned about her grandmother's diagnosis, reliving the day her father died had become an everyday occurrence. If only she'd come straight home from school instead of disobeying her mother and going to the playground with her friends. The thought of her grandmother dying alone in her home, like her father, had consumed her mind. "I don't want to leave you here by yourself."

"I appreciate that, but my life is here. The people in this town have been my family for almost twenty years. I couldn't imagine ever leaving Bluebell." Myrna pulled her hand away and pushed herself from the table. "Jake will be here soon. I better get the icing on these so you can take them with you."

The mention of Jake reminded her of the struggle she had earlier deciding what to wear. She looked down at her black jeans and pink blouse. "Is this outfit okay? I didn't know what to wear. I've never been to a car show." Since Olivia first woke up, she'd had reservations about spending the day with Jake and his children. "Are you sure you can't come with us to the car show? Jake is your friend. I feel uncomfortable going with him and his kids."

"Your outfit is perfect." Myrna glanced at the clock on the wall. She carried the plate of cupcakes and the bowl of icing to the table. "Come and sit with me, dear."

Olivia followed her grandmother and pulled out a chair from the table for each of them. She sat down and took a sip of her coffee.

"Why are you so apprehensive about going to the show with Jake and his children?" Myrna asked as she ran the knife with a glob of vanilla icing over the chocolate cupcake.

"I should have never asked about his wife. I feel terrible. To be honest with you, I didn't remember you mentioning that Jake had lost his wife. I guess I wasn't paying attention. I'm sorry." The coffee soured in Olivia's stomach.

"Don't be so hard on yourself. I never shared the details of what that family has endured with you." Myrna pulled in a slow breath and released it. "It should have been a happy time for Jake's family. His wife, Laura, was seven months pregnant when she went into labor. She had issues with her blood pressure and had a heart attack." Myrna wiped a tear.

"And the baby?"

Her grandmother shook her head. "It devastated Jake. He lost his wife and baby boy in a matter of minutes. If it weren't for his strong faith, I don't think he would have survived."

"That's so sad." Olivia placed her hand over her mouth and shook her head.

"Laura was a wonderful wife and mother. She kept the Beckett house running. Poor Kyle and Kayla, they didn't understand what had happened to their mother. Kyle had terrible nightmares, and Kayla wouldn't talk."

"How did Jake handle it by himself?"

"Oh, he wasn't alone. His brothers were here to support him. Plus, the entire town rallied around him."

Myrna brushed a tear from her cheek.

"After Laura was gone, it paralyzed Jake. The poor guy couldn't operate the washing machine. He didn't know that Kyle liked sliced bananas on his peanut butter sandwich. Or that Kayla won't drink orange juice that has pulp. That was Laura's department. Jake's brothers were there to support him, but the kids needed a mother figure, so I stayed at their house for the first month."

"Why?"

"That's what family does. We support one another. We give our time and effort to someone other than ourselves."

"But you're not family." Olivia couldn't deny feeling a twinge of jealousy. Since the day she'd come home from school and discovered her father nonresponsive on the kitchen floor, all she'd wanted was to be part of a family again.

Myrna reached for Olivia's hand. "It's not blood that makes you family, dear. Love and loyalty bind people together. It's what makes Bluebell Canyon so special. Give it time. You'll see."

Olivia considered her grandmother's words. Olivia's mother had been blood, yet after losing her husband, the only thing her mother seemed to care about was getting her next drink. Had her mother ever considered the effect that finding her father had had on Olivia?

"For weeks, Kyle couldn't fall asleep unless I was in bed with him. Jake and Kyle have come a long way, but Kayla is still in a lot of pain. I think it might be a good thing for her to spend time with you."

"Why would you think that?"

"Let's just say I have a good feeling about the positive effect you could have on her."

Olivia didn't plan to stay in Bluebell Canyon long enough to affect anyone, much less a child who had lost her mother. She still had unresolved issues after losing her father and later being abandoned by her mother. How could she help Kayla? It was clear to her that Jake's circumstances were going to make it more challenging to convince Gammy to come back to Miami.

Outside, car doors slammed. Children's laughter filled the air. Olivia's stomach tightened. It was too late to back out. She'd have to go to the car show with Jake and his kids. It was what Gammy wanted. But after today, Olivia would have to keep her distance from the Beckett family. Getting involved with a grieving widower and his two children wasn't part of her plan. And she certainly didn't want to develop ties to the other townspeople, either. She needed to focus on getting Myrna out of Bluebell Canyon.

Chapter Two

"Every time your grandmother feeds us breakfast, I feel like I've gained ten pounds," Jake joked, to lighten the mood inside his truck. Kyle had been a chatterbox since they'd left Myrna's house. Kayla had barely said a word at breakfast and remained quiet. Olivia sat in the passenger seat with her back ramrod straight, twisting the ends of her hair around her index finger. She stared out the window. The sunlight showcased her creamy complexion. Jake quickly shifted his eyes back to the road as he approached the four-way stop.

"Have you ever attended an antique car show?" Jake raised an eyebrow in Olivia's direction.

"No, I can't say that I have. What exactly happens? Do we drive the cars or go for a ride?"

Kyle's giggles carried from the back seat to the front of the truck's cab. Jake peered in the rearview mirror and saw Kayla rolling her brown eyes.

"Kayla, would you like to explain some car-show etiquette to Dr. Olivia?"

"No."

"I will! I will!" Kyle called out. "Ouch! Stop it, Kay."

"Kids, settle down."

"But, Daddy, Kayla is pinching me."

"Kayla, leave your brother alone. We'll let him explain the protocol to Dr. Olivia."

"There's a certain way to behave?" Olivia questioned.

"Yeah, but it's still fun. You can't touch the cars or lean against them. Stuff like that," Kyle explained. "You need to be respectful of the cars and the owners. They spend a lot of money—" his eyes grew wide "—like a humongous amount to make their cars nice again."

Jake listened to his son with pride. Kyle's mother had grown up going to car shows. Her father had been an enthusiast. Jake and his wife started taking the twins to shows when they were only a year old. Laura made sure as the children got older that they learned the proper etiquette. It was important to her to carry on the tradition she'd shared with her father. Jake couldn't blame Kayla for getting upset that Olivia had joined them. It was difficult for him to have another woman in his wife's seat on a family outing. If Myrna hadn't insisted Olivia join them, he would have never extended the invitation on his own. It didn't feel right.

Olivia looked over her shoulder. "Thank you for educating me." She turned to Kayla. "Is there anything else?"

Kayla stayed quiet while Kyle nodded his head. "Ask a lot of questions. The owners like that."

Olivia smiled. "Okay, I'll remember that. You seem to know a lot about car shows Where did you learn all of this?"

"Our mommy taught us," Kayla responded curtly. "My family went to shows." She crossed her arms. "You're not in our family."

"Kay!"

"What?" Kayla shot a look at her brother. "She's not."

"You don't have to be so mean," Kyle said.

"Your brother is right. I don't like your attitude, young lady." Jake looked at Olivia. "I'm sorry."

Olivia simply nodded.

Jake turned on the radio to extinguish the silence inside the vehicle. The plan to have a nice outing with his children wasn't going as expected. Kayla made it clear she didn't want Olivia to spend the day with them, yet Kyle seemed thrilled. It would be a long day if he didn't turn things around soon.

Thirty minutes later, they arrived at the fairgrounds. A cloud of dust swirled behind the truck as Jake searched for a parking space in the field. "We've got some time before the show starts. Do you want to go on a couple of rides?"

"Yay!" Kyle cheered and pumped his fist. "Kayla and I are tall enough to go on some by ourselves."

The group exited the vehicle. Food trailers lined the trampled path that led to the rides. The smell of popcorn and sugary-sweet funnel cake filled the air. The children took off running and headed toward the merry-go-round.

"Are they okay going by themselves?" Olivia's eyebrow arched.

Jake stuck his hands into the back pockets of his jeans and laughed. "This isn't Miami. We know practically everyone here. That's what makes living in a small town so great."

The twins took their place in line behind two girls who looked to be in their early teens.

"Do you want to have a seat over there?" Jake pointed to a wooden bench underneath an oak tree where he could see the kids and get to know Olivia. He had to try. It might be the only way to convince her how much everyone in Bluebell loved her grandmother.

They sat, and Olivia fingered her necklace and looked toward the children. "I feel like I'm spoiling Kayla's day. I don't think she wants me around."

"Give her time. She's not as comfortable around strangers as Kyle is." Jake wasn't so sure Kayla would soften up to Olivia. He knew his little girl. She was strong-willed when she set her mind to—or against—something. He planned to talk with Kayla tonight at bedtime about being more respectful toward Olivia.

"We didn't exactly get off on the right foot. I shouldn't have made that comment about asking your wife for permission. I'm sorry."

Jake adjusted his cowboy hat to shield the sun from his eyes. "Like I mentioned yesterday, there's no need to apologize. You didn't know."

Olivia resumed twisting her hair around her finger. "I know now. This morning, Gammy told me about Laura and the baby." She dropped her hands and folded them in her lap. "I'm sorry for your loss."

Jake noticed Olivia brushing a tear from her cheek. "Thanks. It's been a rough couple of years." When his wife had gone into distress, they had rushed him out of the delivery room. The staff raced in and out of the room. Jake stood by the door, feeling as if he were float- ing outside of his body. He'd been unable to escape the beeping machines. He knew something wasn't right, yet no one offered to tell him what was happening. When the doctor finally stepped into the hallway, his worst fear became a reality. Laura and the baby hadn't survived. His knees had buckled. He had dropped to the tiled floor. Thoughts of his children coloring in the waiting room with Myrna swirled in his mind. They weren't aware their mother was gone. He thought that taking the children home that night without their mother would be the hardest thing he'd ever do, but telling them what had happened nearly broke him. Jake's eyes scanned over to the children. "Kyle has handled it a little better than Kayla. I think he's trying to be the tough guy."

"Growing up without a mother isn't easy for a young girl," Olivia said.

"Are you speaking from experience?"

"Kind of. I had a wonderful and caring mother, until I lost my father when I was eight." Olivia looked up at the sky.

"I'm sorry." Jake knew Myrna's only son had passed years ago. He didn't recall anything about her son's wife.

Olivia nodded. "After he died, my mother kind of checked out."

"What do you mean?"

Olivia rubbed her palms down her thighs.

"She started drinking…a lot. I was too young to realize she abused alcohol to mask the pain of losing her husband. About a year after he died, my mother left. That's when Gammy and Pops rented out their home down the road from ours in Denver and moved in with me. They stayed until I went off to college. Gammy didn't want me to lose the only home I'd known. For years, no one knew where my mother had gone. There was a part of me that was happy she had left. She wasn't the same person after she started to drink. Once I finished college and moved to Miami, Gammy and Pops sold my childhood home and moved to Bluebell."

"Do you ever hear from your mother?"

Olivia shook her head. "While I was in medical school, my mother died in a car accident."

"Even though she'd been absent from your life, that had to have been tough for you," Jake said.

Olivia paused and turned to Jake. "Really, the day my father died, I lost both parents. If it weren't for Gammy, I don't know what would have happened to me."

"She's a special lady. When my wife passed, your grandmother put her life on hold to help the children and me. She stepped in to help my brothers and took over, starting with the funeral arrangements. I couldn't think straight. I tried to stay strong for Kyle and Kayla, but my heart had shattered." Myrna never pretended to have all the answers. She was simply there during the darkest and most isolating time of his life. Jake had kept sinking further into a depressed state. "Myrna helped put the pieces of our lives back together again. She reminded me to lean on my faith, to look for the light through the darkness." Jake rubbed his eye. "She's an important part of our family."

"I'm glad she was there to help you and the children, but she's my only family and she's an important part of my life, too. That's why I want to help her. I can hire a full-time nurse until I work things out with my job." Olivia turned to Jake. "You saw her yesterday. She couldn't even see the signature line on the papers Larry brought her to sign."

Jake nodded. "I think we can both agree that Myrna's eyes are deteriorating. Over time, she'll need more help."

"So we agree? She shouldn't be living on her own." Olivia straightened her shoulders.

"Hold on a minute. I never said that." Jake didn't like the direction of this conversation.

"Daddy!" Kyle called out. The twins smiled and waved as the merry-go-round powered up. Jake was relieved to see Kayla smiling. His heart squeezed for his little girl, who smiled exactly like her mother.

Jake focused his attention back on the discussion at hand. "I hope you'll hear me out before you decide about moving your grandmother."

"I'll listen, but I can't make any promises."

"Since Myrna's diagnosis, I've been making modifications around the house to make it safer if her eyes worsen."

"I understand and appreciate that, but from what I saw yesterday, it's not a matter of if her eyes get worse. They already are. I don't think she should live alone." Olivia's eyes filled with sadness.

"That's the reason I wanted Myrna to get a service dog." Jake had known it wouldn't take much to convince Myrna. She'd always loved dogs and often had Tank over for sleepovers. Myrna even periodically volunteered with his business when things got too busy with him and his brothers. "At first, she didn't want to admit that she might need help, but she came around. She agreed having a service dog was the best solution to maintain her independence. Remaining independent is very important to her."

Olivia nodded. "I've seen many people come into the ER with service dogs, but I think a nurse would provide better companionship."

"Service animals are excellent companions

and much more." The animals provided their handler with the confidence to get out and continue to live their lives to the fullest. Seeing these dogs change people's lives for the better made his work rewarding.

"Training dogs to assist people with disabilities is an admirable business."

Jake couldn't imagine doing any other type of work. "Thank you. It's wonderful to see the hard work pay off when the dog graduates and meets their new handler."

"Yesterday, you mentioned a camp for Puppy Raisers. What's that?"

"Puppy Raisers are individuals who commit to fostering a potential guide or service dog puppy in their home for the first year of the dog's life before formal training can begin."

"Interesting. I'd like to hear more."

Olivia was showing interest. This was good.

"My goal with Camp Bow Wow is to socialize and educate the puppy about everyday life and outdoor experiences while training the animals to work and perform tasks for people with disabilities. I expose the puppy to things they'd encounter working as a service dog, so they become comfortable and confident in any situation. For example, they visit grocery stores and restaurants, and learn how to behave and help their owners in all potential real-life scenarios. We meet Monday through Friday from three thirty to five thirty for three weeks. These hours allow the twins to help. I want them to see how blessed they are and to have compassion toward the disabled. After camp is over, I do follow-ups by video and make myself available to answer questions."

"Do all the puppies enrolled in your camp advance to train as service animals?"

"Usually, but now and then, we have a dog owner interested in training their own dog. The current group is all volunteer Puppy Raisers who will give up their dog after a year. Our business usually works with breeders who have ancestry lines that have proved to be successful in the past with specific disabilities. It's important to keep in mind that not every puppy is cut out to work as a service animal. That doesn't mean they'll make a bad pet. They just don't have what it takes to provide the critical support required of a service dog."

"Is Callie enrolled in your camp?"

Jake smiled. "Yes, but Callie is what you might call a work in progress. She's been a slow learner, but your grandmother fell in love with her the first time they met. I'll admit, I haven't had a lot of time to work with Callie, but I think she'll be a great help to Myrna."

"Did you get her through one of your breeders?"

"No, a local veteran named George Waters rescued Callie from a shelter in Denver when Callie was two months old. He planned to be her Puppy Raiser, but then he got sick and passed away. When he was diagnosed with cancer, he asked that I go forward with training Callie. I mentioned Myrna might need help in the future because of her recent diagnosis of macular degeneration. Since he and Myrna were good friends, he insisted I train Callie to help Myrna. I promised George I would carry out his request."

"So, you're training Callie to be Gammy's eyes?"

Jake nodded. "Myrna could live independently for years to come." Maintaining Myrna's independence—and keeping her and her friendship close—was Jake's goal.

"What if I take over as Callie's Puppy Raiser? Then she could get used to living with Gammy. I could help you train Callie. You said yourself that you've been busy."

Jake hadn't expected this from Olivia. With a hectic schedule at the hospital, he figured she'd be more likely to own a cat since they could be less maintenance. "Do you like dogs? I don't require my Raisers to have experience training, but they must have a love for dogs."

"Who doesn't love puppies?" Olivia smiled.

"Callie won't stay a puppy forever. A fully grown golden retriever can be quite large."

"I'm familiar with the breed. I think Callie and I will get along fine."

"It takes an enormous commitment. It would be your responsibility to oversee the care of Callie, like feeding, grooming, socialization and exercising. Do you think you'd have the time?"

"I've taken a sabbatical from my job with no set return date, so I can stay as long as it takes to get Callie trained. By then, I'll be able to better assess whether it's in my grandmother's best interest to stay in Bluebell or move to Miami and live with me."

Didn't Myrna get a say in the matter? Of course, that was between Olivia and her grandmother, so he held his peace on the subject. "Okay then." He extended his hand and gave a single nod. "It's a deal. We'll work together to get Callie trained if you agree to hold off on any decision about moving Myrna."

Olivia accepted Jake's hand. "All right, but Callie must prove to me that Gammy will be safe living independently."

Jake glanced up at the sun and released a slow and steady breath. Maybe having Olivia along today hadn't been such a bad idea. "I'll bring Callie over after church tomorrow so you can meet her." Once Olivia got firsthand experience with the service a trained dog could provide, she'd feel much more at ease with Myrna staying in Bluebell. At least, that was what he was hoping for. But not just for himself—for Kyle and Kayla. It would devastate them if Myrna moved away.

"Daddy, Daddy! Come quick!"

Jake's eyes shot toward the sound of Kyle's frantic cry. He sprang from the bench and bolted toward Kayla. Arms and legs flailed in all directions as Kayla rolled on the ground with a girl he'd seen in the line earlier.

"Ouch! My hair!" Kayla yelled.

"Kayla! Stop!" Jake reached down to pull his daughter off the other girl, who appeared older and bigger than Kayla.

"Let me go!" Kayla squirmed in Jake's arms.

Another girl who'd been in the line ran to the scene. "Come on, Lisa. Just say you're sorry. We have to go meet Aunt Jane at the concession stand."

"Would either of you care to explain what this is about?" Jake asked as Olivia joined the group.

Neither child said a word.

"I was talking to Jeremy, so I don't know what happened. I came back, and they were rolling around on the ground, pulling hair and stuff." Kyle spoke up.

Jake glanced at his son before addressing the

girls. "Lisa, I think I know everyone in town, but I can't say I recall ever seeing you before."

"We're visiting our aunt Jane." Lisa's voice shook.

"Jane McWilliams?"

Lisa nodded and brushed her hair from her face.

"Okay, so do you want to tell me your side of the story?" Jake asked.

Lisa nodded. "We were waiting in line to go on the merry-go-round again. I said her mother was pretty. When I turned around, she jumped on me and punched me."

"Stop saying that!" Kayla lunged toward Lisa. "She's not my mother! She's not my mother!" Kayla wailed and pointed.

"Whoa, hold on." Jake reached for Kayla's arm before she could tackle Lisa once again. Kayla's body was stiff. Jake had never seen her this way. "Kayla, you need to calm down."

Jake turned in the direction Kayla was pointing. Olivia. He should have known. Lisa thought Olivia was Kayla's mother. A lump formed in his throat. He scooped up Kayla. Her torso went limp as she surrendered her tears.

"It's okay, sweetie." Jake stroked the back of Kayla's head.

"It's never going to be okay without my mommy."

"I'm sorry." Lisa looked up at Jake. "I didn't mean to make her cry."

Jake gave an understanding nod. "I know you didn't. Kayla shouldn't have lashed out at you. I'm sorry. I hope you and your sister can forgive her."

Lisa nodded.

"Let's go." Lisa's sister took her sibling's hand, and they walked away.

"I miss my mommy." Kayla's lip quivered as she buried her face into Jake's shoulder. His knees nearly buckled.

Olivia kept her distance to give Kayla space.

Jake hated to disappoint Kyle, but he had to take Kayla home. "I think we better forget the car show."

"But, Daddy!" Kyle whimpered. "You promised."

"I'm sorry, buddy, but your sister is upset. I think it's best if we go home."

"I want to see Miss Myrna." Kayla whimpered.

Kyle kicked his boot into the ground, stirring up a puff of dirt. "It's not fair."

Tension grew in Jake's neck, but he knew what he had to do. Myrna was the only one capable of calming Kayla down.

"Maybe I can stay here and take Kyle to the show," Olivia offered.

Kyle's eyes brightened. "Yes! Please, Daddy!" Jake considered Olivia's offer.

"Let her stay. I don't want to ride in the car with her," Kayla whispered. Jake looked at Olivia, hoping she hadn't heard Kayla's request. It wasn't Olivia's fault, just like it wasn't Lisa's fault, either. Both were innocent victims of Kayla's grief.

"Are you sure you want to do that? You didn't seem too thrilled about the car show from the start." Jake tried to give Olivia an easy out.

Olivia looked at Kyle and smiled. "Actually, after listening to Kyle, I think we'll have a great time."

Kyle flew toward Olivia and wrapped his arms around her waist. "We'll have fun, Dr. Olivia! I promise!" Kyle turned back to his father. "Can me and Dr. Olivia still have a picnic and see the fireworks?"

How could he disappoint Kyle? Jake glanced at his watch. "It's not quite lunchtime."

"Maybe Kyle and I can walk back to the truck with you. I saw some picnic tables close to where you parked. We can take our sandwiches and hang out for a little while," Olivia suggested.

Kyle grinned. "Don't forget Miss Myrna's cupcakes."

Jake laughed. "I won't, but you might need to

skip the fireworks this year, buddy." Having lunch and taking Kyle to the car show for a couple of hours were one thing, but staying for the fireworks would make a long day for Olivia.

"But we always stay and watch. Why do we always have to do what Kayla wants?" Kyle rolled his lower lip and crossed his arms across his chest.

"We can stay for the fireworks. I'd love to see them." Olivia placed her hand on Kyle's shoulder. "Kyle and I will have a great time."

Kayla buried her head deeper into Jake's shoulder.

"Can we, Daddy?" Kyle pleaded.

The thought of having both of his children upset was more than he could handle. "Okay, I'll come back to pick you up later. Maybe by then Kayla will change her mind and want to watch the fireworks."

"No! I want to stay with Miss Myrna." Kayla stiffened.

"If it's all right with Myrna, I'll come back to catch the fireworks with you two." Watching the incredible light show had always been his wife's favorite way to close a perfect day. Of course, today had been anything but perfect. Given Kayla's feelings toward Olivia, Jake wondered if working with the doctor to train Callie was asking for more trouble.

* * *

"Are you sure the pressure cooker is okay, Gammy? Look at it shake. I think it's going to blow its top." Olivia covered her eyes and retreated from the pot. When she was a little girl, her mother had tried to cook in one of these. After her father arrived home from work, the pot blew its lid. Black beans exploded all over the room. A few even stuck to the ceiling. Olivia never saw her father laugh that hard again. A few weeks later, he passed away. She brushed off the reminder that the only two men she'd ever loved had left her with a broken heart.

"The green beans are fine, dear. That's what it's supposed to do." Myrna wiped her hands down the front of her apron. "Did you and Kyle have fun yesterday?"

Spending the day with Kyle had filled her heart with joy. "I don't remember when I've had a better day."

Gammy's eyes shifted to Olivia.

"That makes me happy. You work too much. Life's short. You need to slow down and enjoy the moment. Trust me. It goes fast. I don't want you to have any regrets when you're my age."

Olivia considered her grandmother's words. When she and Mark were first married, Olivia thought they'd have at least two children. In the early years, she couldn't put all the blame on her husband. Olivia was beginning her career. She thought there'd be time for children. But at thirty-six and single again, it felt like time was running out. The one thing she wanted more than anything was to have a family. But how could she trust another man after Mark had revealed he didn't want children after all? "I'll be fine."

"I know Mark changed his mind about having children, but that doesn't mean you don't have other options. Have you considered adoption?"

Olivia had plenty of friends who had adopted children, but they were married. Olivia wanted a family like she'd had before her father died and her mother turned to alcohol. "Unless I changed my schedule, raising a child on my own would be difficult."

"Keep your options open, dear. You could always marry a man who already has children."

Olivia couldn't ignore the twinkle in Gammy's eyes.

"Speaking of, did you enjoy the fireworks? I'm happy Jake joined you and Kyle for the show."

Her grandmother's motives were becoming questionable. "Yes, we had a wonderful time." Olivia had only wished Kayla had been with them.

The timer on the oven beeped. Olivia was thankful for the interruption.

"Can you get the biscuits?"

Olivia grabbed the pot holders and opened the door. She removed the cookie sheet and placed the tray on the trivet. "Since you were asleep when I got home from the car show, I wasn't able to tell you what Jake and I discussed."

"Jake phoned this morning and filled me in on your plans to work together to train Callie. I'm excited to have the dog here full-time. You're going to love her. Over the years, I've met many of the Puppy Raisers. I think this might be what you need."

"What do you mean?"

Myrna removed the lid from the slow cooker. The savory aroma of succulent beef and vegetables mixed in a spicy broth filled the air. "Between working long hours and the stress you were under during the divorce, maybe it's time to reevaluate your life."

"And you think training a puppy is the answer?" Olivia laughed.

"I'll let you come to your own conclusion over the coming weeks." Myrna replaced the lid. "The pot roast is nearly ready." She glanced at her watch. "Jake and the kids should be here any minute."

Olivia's suspicions mounted. "Did you invite Jake and the kids to dinner because of me? If you're trying to play matchmaker with the car show and dinners, it won't work." Olivia needed to put a stop to this. Sure, Jake was gorgeous, and he seemed nice enough, but putting her trust in another man wasn't in her plans right now, or perhaps ever. Her heart couldn't handle more pain. Besides, one of his two children probably wouldn't mind if she dropped off the face of the earth.

"I'm doing no such thing. I've had Jake and the children over for Sunday supper since Laura died."

Olivia's cheeks warmed. "I'm sorry. I didn't mean to be disrespectful. I just need time to myself."

"Don't take too much time alone, dear. Like I said earlier, you have options. You don't want to put it off too long. Raising children takes a lot of energy."

"I can't jump and marry a man because I want children."

"No, but you could keep your heart open to the possibility. My grandmother always said there's a lid for every kettle. You'll find your lid."

"We're here!" Kyle's voice carried through the house.

Olivia turned to the sound of the front door opening. Dogs barked, and toenails skittered on the hardwood floor, rapidly approaching the kitchen.

A loud crash sounded.

"Oops! Sorry, Miss Myrna," Kyle called out. "Callie knocked over your plant stand."

Gammy didn't seem fazed by all the commotion. Olivia questioned if she could handle the dog. She raised her eyebrow at her grandmother. "This is okay with you?"

Myrna turned the setting on the slow cooker to warm and wiped her hands with the dishcloth. "I wouldn't have it any other way. Go grab the dustpan and broom from the pantry. Let's get it cleaned up so we can eat dinner."

Myrna pivoted on her heels and exited the kitchen.

Olivia sprinted from the pantry at the sound of more breaking glass.

Once in the living room, Olivia noticed the toppled plant stand had sent shards of broken porcelain and dirt all over the floor. The Oriental rug was a mess.

"Kids, grab the dogs and take them outside until we get this cleaned up. And put Callie on a leash so she doesn't run off," Jake instructed. "I'll get the other broom from the garage."

Olivia directed her attention to Jake. "Is she always like this?"

"Tank gets her riled up. Like I mentioned yesterday, Callie has a lot to learn."

"Obviously," Olivia mumbled.

"If Callie is going to live here full-time, we'll need to doggy proof the house. That will involve removing easily accessible items from dressers, tables and countertops. You don't want to leave things like shoes, socks, clothing, medications, chemicals, electrical cords or food lying around. If there are rooms where you'd rather Callie didn't enter, then I'd recommend you close the door or put up a baby gate. It's better to be safe than sorry." Jake spun around and headed toward the garage.

Olivia scanned the area. There was potting soil strewn over the floor and a second plant knocked over. "How did that one fall? It's on top of the end table."

Myrna laughed. "When puppies get excited, they like to jump. Like Jake said, if Callie can reach it, then move it."

"Look at this mess." Olivia went to work with the broom.

"You need to loosen up a bit, dear. Real life is messy. Everything doesn't have to be neat and organized," Myrna stated.

Olivia bit her lower lip. Gammy was right. She'd lost her joy when she discovered her father unconscious on the kitchen floor. In the years that followed, she'd buried her grief and replaced it with a determination to carry out her father's legacy to become a prominent doctor.

Did her ex-husband believe she'd never make time for children? Was she the reason he'd changed his mind about having kids?

Chapter Three

"Okay, I think we're all done here. Everything seems to be back in its place." Jake swept the last pile of dirt and broken glass onto the dustpan.

Olivia placed her hands on her hips. "What about Gammy's plants? The dogs destroyed them."

"I'll replace them. It's not like this hasn't happened before." Jake chuckled and looked at Myrna. "Right?"

Myrna nodded. "Remember the first time you brought Tank over to the house? He snatched the rib-eye steak from the countertop and ran all over the house. It took us twenty minutes to get our hands on him."

"I remember. He'd hidden under the guest room bed, and by the time we found him, all that was left was bone," Jake recalled. It was the first time since losing his wife that he'd laughed.

"Well, nothing like that will happen to Callie. I'll have her house-trained in no time," Olivia said.

"Yeah, right," Kayla mumbled from the corner of the living room.

Jake focused his attention on his daughter. Her tears from yesterday had faded, but her attitude toward Olivia remained. "Didn't I tell you last night if you don't have something nice to say, hold your peace?"

"But, Daddy, you said Callie was difficult and training dogs is your job." Kayla frowned at Olivia. "She's probably never been around one. You always say to be a Puppy Raiser, you have to love dogs."

Jake watched Olivia's face flush. When he'd told the kids Olivia would help train Callie, Kyle had been ecstatic. Kayla had run out of the room in tears.

Myrna moved toward Kayla and placed her hand on her shoulder. "You've helped your father with other Puppy Raisers. Maybe you can help Dr. Olivia, Kayla. She doesn't have a dog of her own, but I know she's always loved animals."

"I can help, too!" Kyle raced toward the two women and bounced up and down. "I'm pretty responsible. I put Callie and Tank in the fenced area before we came inside."

Jake smiled. "Good thinking, son."

Kyle straightened his shoulders.

"She doesn't want my help. I don't think she likes kids, either." Kayla shrugged Myrna's hand away.

"Stop being so mean." Kyle frowned at his sister.

Jake approached his daughter. "That's enough, young lady."

"But she's old, and she doesn't even have any kids." Kayla's words rolled quickly off her tongue.

"I don't know where you left your manners today, but I believe you owe Dr. Olivia an apology."

"Sorry." Kayla kept her eyes focused on the floor and crossed her arms.

Olivia nodded.

An awkward silence hung in the air. Outside, the only train that crossed through the town sounded its whistle.

"Let's all take a deep breath and go have our dinner. I've made your favorite, Kayla, pot roast with baby carrots." Myrna motioned her arms toward the kitchen.

"Can we go outside after we eat?" Kyle asked. "I can show Dr. Olivia some stuff that might help her with Callie. Kayla can help, too."

Jake glanced in Olivia's direction. Sadness

filled her eyes. Yesterday, Jake could excuse Kayla's actions toward Olivia, since the car show was her mother's favorite family activity. The day had stirred memories for Kayla, but today was a new day and her behavior was inexcusable. He'd discuss her punishment once they got home. Jake was proud of his son for trying to be the peacemaker. "I think that's a great idea."

Myrna stooped in front of Kayla. "You're good with Tank. Maybe you can show Dr. Olivia a few things."

A tiny smile parted Kayla's lips. "Okay."

Jake's shoulders relaxed. He would never have been able to convince Kayla to help Olivia. Myrna had a special touch with his daughter.

"I'll race you to the kitchen, Kay!" Kyle yelled. Kayla accepted his challenge and took off running. Myrna followed the children.

Olivia kept her feet firmly planted.

"Are you ready to eat?" Jake stepped closer and noticed the scent of lavender surrounding Olivia.

"I do like children. I guess I'm just not comfortable around them." Olivia twirled a strand of her hair. "I don't have experience with kids, except in the ER."

"Kayla's behavior toward you is unacceptable. I'll be sure and speak with her when we get home later."

"Don't be too hard on her."

Jake ran his hand across his chin. "Sometimes I feel like I can't do anything right as far as Kayla is concerned. Your grandmother is so good with her. Myrna always knows exactly what to say to make her feel better."

"Is that your subtle way of saying Gammy should remain in Bluebell Canyon?"

"I'd like that, but it wasn't what I meant. Besides, you agreed to postpone any decision until we get Callie trained and I finish more of the home modifications. I have some great ideas that I'd like to run by you."

"I'm sorry. You're right." Olivia nodded. "Thank you for offering to share the improvements you'd like to do on Gammy's home. I appreciate it. Maybe I could help you with them."

"I can always use an extra hand." Jake smiled. "I'm starving. What do you say we head back to the kitchen and get something to eat before the kids devour everything?"

"I'll be there in a minute." Olivia slid her hands into the back pockets of her jeans.

Jake walked away, leaving Olivia alone in the living room. He sent up a silent prayer that going forward everyone would work together for the shared goal of helping Myrna.

* * *

Later, with their stomachs full, Jake and Olivia headed outside with the children. Olivia offered to help Myrna, but she insisted cleaning the kitchen was relaxing and something she preferred to do alone.

The late-afternoon sun peeked through the large oak trees lining Myrna's property.

"Come over here." Kyle reached for Olivia's hand and led her toward the fenced area where Tank relaxed in the shade. Callie circled the property, looking for a way to escape.

Kyle looked up at Olivia and squinted. "The most important thing you need to remember is that puppies are hyper."

Olivia laughed. "Is that so?"

"Tell her, Daddy."

"Kyle's right, but she'll grow out of that stage. Eventually you won't have to worry about her running through the house destroying things like you saw earlier. But for now, we need to keep things out of her reach."

"Has she been potty trained?" Olivia asked.

"She is now. When George rescued Callie, he learned that was the reason she'd ended up in the shelter." Jake never understood people who purchased puppies but didn't have the patience to put in the time required to train them properly. "It's one of the main reasons dogs end up in shelters. People don't want to come home from a long day at work to find their flooring or rugs destroyed, but they won't train their pet."

Olivia glanced between Jake and Kyle. "Isn't having accidents a given for a new puppy?"

"It doesn't have to be if the owner puts in the effort. But it doesn't end after the animal is potty trained. Dogs need exercise, especially service dogs," Jake explained.

"That's not a problem." Olivia shrugged her shoulders. "If Gammy and Callie end up coming home with me, there are several dog parks near my condo in Miami."

Jake laughed.

Olivia directed her gaze at Jake. "What's so funny?"

"Taking Callie out once a day for a walk in the dog park won't cut it. Puppies can go all day long. By nightfall, they'll still have the same energy they had from the start of the day. In addition, pups must have exposure to a variety of indoor and outdoor sounds, especially if they are to become a service animal."

"Why is that necessary?"

"This is something we cover in camp, but have you ever tried running a vacuum cleaner near a puppy?"

Olivia shook her head.

"Whether a vacuum, a lawn mower or a leaf

blower, motorized tools can terrify a puppy and result in a fight-or-flight reaction. It's important they have repeated exposure in order to become accustomed to the noises. In time, the puppy will learn it is safe as long as it has a history of being safe around it."

"I never realized there was so much involved with training a dog."

Jake nodded. "Most people don't." He looked across the yard. "Come here, boy!"

Immediately, Tank was up and running toward Jake. Once at his feet, Jake reached down and scratched the dog behind his ear. "Tank might not be a puppy, but he benefits from outdoor activities like most dogs." Jake pushed his hands into his back pockets.

"I'm fairly active, so I'm sure I won't have any trouble keeping up with Callie," Olivia explained.

Kyle looked up at his father. "I don't think she understands."

Jake shrugged his shoulders. He couldn't say he hadn't warned Olivia. He hoped in time, she'd realize the effort and patience that were necessary to train a puppy. "I'm going to run inside and get their food. It's time for the dogs to have their dinner. Keep your eyes on her, kids."

"Dr. Olivia or Callie?" Kayla questioned.

"Both." Jake winked and jogged inside the house.

"How's it going out there?" Myrna called out over her shoulder as she rinsed the dinner plates.

"I'm afraid Olivia doesn't realize training Callie won't be easy. I know she's a doctor, but I'm not sure she understands the time and energy required to be a Puppy Raiser."

Myrna turned off the faucet and dried her hands on the dish towel. "I think she got a little taste of it earlier," she said with a smile.

"Believe it or not, Callie has settled down a bit since I've gotten her into a routine. She's rowdy when she's first let out of the car, but at least she hasn't gotten her teeth into my wallet again." After Callie had chewed up a one-hundred-dollar bill, Jake learned quickly to keep his wallet in his nightstand drawer.

"I'm happy Olivia wants to be a Puppy Raiser and help with Callie's training at Camp Bow Wow." Myrna smiled.

Jake hoped that after Callie completed her training, Olivia would see firsthand how much Callie could help her grandmother. "So am I, but best of all, she said she will put off deciding on moving you until I have time to finish the modifications to your home and see how things progress with Callie."

"That sounds promising, but don't worry

about me leaving Bluebell." Myrna swatted her hand in the air. "That will never happen."

"Daddy!" Kyle raced through the kitchen door.

"What is it? Is Kayla hurt?" Jake's pulse quickened.

Kyle blinked rapidly. "No! It's Callie. Dr. Olivia accidentally put her outside the fence without her leash. Callie took off like a rocket ship."

"Oh, dear." Myrna placed her hand against the side of her face.

"Hurry, Daddy!" Kyle cried out.

"You and your sister stay here and feed Tank. I'll go after Callie. Don't worry. I'll find her." Jake sprinted out the door and right past Olivia.

"Jake, I'm sorry!" Olivia yelled. "Let me help!"

Jake ignored the apology and her offer to help. He had to find Callie. He increased his pace as he neared the steep hill. On the other side were deep woods, and with the cloud cover that had moved in, it would be dark soon. Jake pumped his arms as he neared the top of the hill. If Callie continued into the wooded area, finding her would be impossible.

"Dear, please sit down and have some tea. Jake will find Callie. He knows those woods inside and out."

Olivia continued to pace the wraparound

porch. The moment Callie had taken off, guilt had consumed her mind. Jake had warned her about removing Callie's leash. Her eyes scanned the property. The wildflowers covering the fields were quickly fading into the shadows. Olivia shuddered to think what could happen if it got too dark to keep searching for the puppy. "What if he doesn't? I'll never forgive myself if something happens to her."

"Relax. You worry too much. Jake will find her."

Myrna stood up from the rocking chair and picked up the teakettle from the side table. She filled a cup and placed it on a saucer. "Here, drink this. It's chamomile. It will calm your nerves."

Olivia accepted the beverage and sat on the edge of the rocker. A brisk breeze whooshed up the porch steps and caused a shiver to move down her spine. *Callie is too small to be off on her own. What if there are coyotes in the area? Why in the world did I remove the leash knowing Callie isn't trained?*

"Miss Myrna!" Kyle called out as he and Kayla raced through the yard and scaled the steps. Tank trailed behind, secured on a leash. "It's almost dark. Do you think we should take Daddy's truck and look for Callie? He keeps the key under the floor mat." Kyle sank into the empty rocking chair. Tank plopped on the floor beside him.

Olivia didn't have to look in Kayla's direction. She could feel the child's eyes burning into the side of her face. This was all her fault. "That sounds like a good idea. I could drive."

Kayla crossed her arms. "You'll make it worse."

"Kayla! Didn't your father tell you to hold your peace if you don't have something nice to say?" Myrna asked.

"Yeah, Kay. Dr. Olivia can't help it if she doesn't know anything about puppies. She's not a dog doctor. Besides, maybe Daddy should have used the crate from his truck to keep Callie from running loose."

"Isn't that cruel to lock a dog up in a cage?" Olivia asked.

Kayla rolled her eyes.

Myrna motioned for the child. "Come over here and sit with me. I think we all need to relax and take a deep breath. There's no point in us rushing off to help with the search. Your father will be back with Callie any minute. We just have to be patient."

Kayla's shoulders slumped and her lower lip rolled as she crossed the porch. "What if Callie is gone forever?" Kayla climbed on Myrna's lap and nuzzled her face against the woman's shoulder.

Myrna's phone rang. Olivia hoped it was good news.

Following a brief exchange, her grandmother ended the call and slid the phone into the pocket of her apron. "That was Jake."

"Did he find Callie?" the twins asked in unison.

"Yes, and she's fine. So you can stop worrying. Why don't you two run inside and start working on that jigsaw puzzle you dumped on the dining room table? I'll be along to help you in a minute."

All smiles, the children hurried into the house. The screen door closed with a bang.

Olivia released a slow and steady breath. "I'm glad Jake found Callie safe." Despite the good news, her grandmother looked concerned. "What is it? Did you say Callie was okay for the children's sake?"

"No, it's Jake I'm worried about."

"What's wrong?"

Myrna stepped toward the screen door. "I don't want the children to hear. After losing their mother, they're so afraid something will happen to their father—especially Kayla."

Olivia understood. After her father died, she raced home from school each day to ensure her mother was okay, especially after her mother started abusing alcohol. Olivia's heart would pound in her chest as she got closer to the kitchen. Flashes of her father on the floor would replay in her mind. For months leading up to her mother leaving, Olivia refused to go out and play with her friends, afraid that something would happen to her mother.

Myrna pulled the door closed, silencing the laughter echoing through the foyer. "I need you to drive to the Pearsons' ranch and pick up Jake and Callie."

"Of course. I can do that." With the sun setting soon, Olivia assumed it might be too far to walk.

"Jake twisted his ankle. He says it's no big deal, but I think you should check for broken bones. Ronnie can't drive him and Callie back here because the truck he uses to putter around the ranch has a dead battery and his wife took their SUV to visit her ill sister."

"Don't worry. I'll pick them up." Olivia ran inside to grab her car keys.

Ten minutes after Olivia left her grandmother's house, the sun had set as she navigated the vehicle down the winding road. With assistance from the high beam headlights, she spotted a two-story farmhouse with a large wraparound porch up ahead. She often dreamed of a home like this. With children chasing each other around the property while a dog nipped at their

heels. Her shoulders slumped at her current reality. Her home in Miami was empty.

Olivia arrived at the end of the driveway and
two porch lights turned on. She placed the vehicle into Park. A door slammed while she fumbled with her seat belt. Olivia looked up and
spotted Jake.

She exited the car and released a sigh of relief
when Jake approached with the puppy nestled
in his muscular arms. Her heart pumped a little
faster. What was it about a man with a puppy?

"Your grandmother sure is stubborn. I told
her I could walk back. I'm sorry to trouble you."
Jake lifted his foot and gave it a shake. "It feels
fine now."

"You know Gammy. She never takes no for
an answer." Olivia looked down. "Are you sure
your ankle is okay?"

"Not even a limp." Jake gave a reassuring
nod.

"That's good to hear, but you still might want
to ice it once you're home."

"Okay, Doc." Jake saluted.

"How's Callie?" Olivia moved toward the animal and scratched her head.

"She's fine, but she'll sleep well tonight. For
being so young, she covered a lot of ground."
Jake secured the leash around Callie's collar before placing her back on the ground.

"I'm sorry I took Callie off the leash." Olivia gazed at the animal. "If anything had happened to her, I would have never forgiven myself. Please, I hope you'll accept my apology."

Jake nodded. "There's no need to apologize. I should have crated her, so let's forget about it. The important thing is that we work together to get Callie trained, so that she can assist Myrna." Jake looked down at Callie. "Are you ready to go home?"

Callie jumped to her feet and barked.

Jake turned to Olivia. "I think she's hungry. Let's head home."

Olivia took quick, shallow breaths as they headed toward the SUV. Why did the thought of being alone in the car with Jake suddenly make her nervous?

Once inside, they both secured their seat belts. A spicy, masculine scent filled the air. Whatever their disagreements were about moving her grandmother, she couldn't deny the man was easy on the eyes. Way too easy.

Chapter Four

Tuesday afternoon, Olivia squinted against the sun's light as her SUV crested the top of the hill. With the window cracked, she inhaled the crisp air while taking in the picturesque scenery of the Rocky Mountain range, the complete opposite of the views in Miami. The sight of the palm trees that lined the Florida streets had always calmed her nerves, but there was no disputing that the Sunshine State was almost shockingly flat compared to Colorado.

From the back of the car, Callie whined three times and then started to bark nonstop. She obviously wasn't happy to be inside the crate.

"Settle down, Callie," Olivia called out over her shoulder. She pushed away a strand of hair that had escaped her ponytail. The dog wasn't the only one who was nervous. Thinking about spending the afternoon with Jake at Camp Bow

Wow had Olivia's nerves rattled all morning. At least there would be other Puppy Raisers in attendance to keep her from being distracted by Jake's rugged good looks. She needed to focus on Callie.

Cruising down the winding dirt road, Olivia slowed the vehicle to steal a glance at the handwritten map lying on the passenger seat. She chuckled at the map Gammy had drawn for her. It triggered childhood memories of the maps she and her friends drew when they played treasure hunt.

About a mile and a half back, Olivia had made a turn off the main road, but she hadn't yet spotted any houses. According to Gammy, Jake's two younger brothers and business partners, Cody and Logan, lived on the massive plot of land they'd inherited years ago. It was divided into several parcels with five homes. A third brother, Luke, a retired professional bull rider, lived in Virginia with his family, but he maintained a residence on the farm. Jake's father also had a house on the land, but he resided in Denver to be close to his wife, who was in late-stage Alzheimer's. The family had cared for Mrs. Beckett at home, even providing her with a trained companion service dog. But in the end, she needed the professional care of doctors and nurses not available in Bluebell. Their father believed moving her to a nursing home was best for his wife. Jake had a close-knit family, something Olivia always dreamed of for her future. But was Gammy right? Had she allowed her job to consume her to where it may become the only future she could have?

Callie barked twice and released a whimper.

"I know. You're ready to get some exercise." On Sunday, Jake had given Olivia a flight kennel to transport Callie in the car. It was a plastic cage, but smaller than the crate he planned to give her today at Callie's first day at Camp Bow Wow. "We should be at Jake's any minute."

Callie's nails scraped incessantly against the plastic.

Olivia bit her lower lip. "I forgot to let you go to the bathroom before we left the house. Is that it?"

Callie barked.

"Was that a yes?" Olivia laughed.

Another bark echoed inside the vehicle. Olivia eased her foot off the accelerator and hit the brake. "All right, we'll make a quick pit stop, but you'll have to hurry. We don't want to be late for your first day of camp. I have a feeling the instructor doesn't appreciate tardiness."

Olivia stepped from the car and quickly rounded to the back passenger door. The tantalizing aroma of wildflowers decorating the open field along the road scented the air. She reached inside the car and gripped the plastic latch of the kennel. "What in the world?" Callie's wet tongue covered her hands, making it difficult for Olivia to unlock it. "Hang on. I'll have you out in a second."

Finally, the lock released. Olivia opened the sliding door and lifted Callie from the kennel. She squirmed and kicked her hind legs.

"Wait just a second. I need to get your leash," Olivia pleaded as Callie's head butted against her chin.

Callie continued to wiggle. Her sharp toenails pierced Olivia's arms. "Ouch! Settle down, Callie." With one powerful jolt, the animal escaped from Olivia's grasp. She hit the ground and took off running.

"Wait!" Olivia's heart hammered against her chest.

The thought of running after Callie crossed her mind, but the dog had already nearly covered an entire football field. Seizing her on foot would be impossible. Olivia pivoted on her heel and hurried back to the driver's side of the car. Once inside, she pushed the ignition button, fastened her seat belt and peered through the windshield. Between the glaring sunlight and the film on the glass, she struggled to see. Since the dirt road wasn't parallel to the field, the chances of finding Callie by car seemed as hopeless as traveling on foot. How could she face Jake? What would she tell him? In nearly forty-eight hours, she'd lost Callie for the second time. Perspiration peppered her forehead. Olivia jammed her foot on the accelerator, kicking up a cloud of dust. There was no way she could show up at the camp without Callie. What kind of Puppy Raiser lost her dog on the first training day?

"Look, Daddy!" Kyle ran from the inside of the barn and pointed. "It's Callie."

Jake pulled his attention from his iPad and shielded his eyes from the sun. He spotted Callie across the north pasture, racing toward the barn.

"Oh, man. Dr. Olivia let her off the leash again." Kayla rolled her eyes.

Jake wasn't sure what had happened. Olivia had agreed to bring Callie to the camp, but he'd expected they would arrive together.

As Callie approached, the four other puppies enrolled in the camp rose to their hind legs and barked. The Puppy Raisers held tight to their leashes.

Callie ran to Jake and jumped up and down before flopping on the ground at his feet. "How did you get here?" Jake bent over and scooped up the dog. He ran his fingers through Callie's coat. "Run and grab a leash, Kyle."

Kyle sprinted to the barn and returned with the leather strap.

Jake secured Callie's collar and glanced at his watch. "Kayla, why don't you handle Callie so we don't hold up the class?"

"Okay, Daddy." Kayla took the leash and joined the group.

Jake moved inside the center of the orange cones that formed a large circle. He scanned the group and sent up a silent prayer, giving thanks for these dedicated volunteers. "Since we have already been chatting online in the Puppy Raiser group, I won't waste your time with introductions. Thanks for being here. As a Puppy Raiser, your role is critical and the first step your puppy will need if he or she will advance to formal service dog training." Jake turned to the youngest in the group. "Rebecca, this is your third puppy, isn't it?"

Rebecca stepped forward with her golden retriever. "Yes, this is Honey. My other two puppies were Labradors. This is my first golden. Being a Puppy Raiser has been a rewarding experience. It's hard to say goodbye to your puppy once they are ready to train to become a service dog, but knowing I've helped to make a difference in someone's life makes it all worth it."

The group broke into applause. Jake smiled. He was proud of Rebecca. She took her role as a Puppy Raiser seriously, as did most of the volunteers.

"Thank you for sharing with us, Rebecca. That's exactly the reason my brothers and I started this academy. The goal of Camp Bow Wow is to teach each puppy about trust, bravery, basic obedience, socialization and love. These skills will give them the foundation to eventually, with further training, become service dogs if that's your goal. Many enroll in the camp to train their family pet."

Off in the distance, tires crunched along the gravel road. Before Jake saw the vehicle, he knew it was Olivia.

"There's Dr. Olivia's car!" Kyle pointed to the SUV cresting the hill.

"She's driving way too fast!" Kayla yelled.

Jake shot his daughter a look. "Remember what I told you about holding your tongue?"

"But she is!"

The SUV came to a screeching halt, stirring up a cloud of dust. Olivia haphazardly parked her vehicle in the lot next to the barn. She sprang from the car and raced toward the group. "Callie got away from me again." Olivia stopped long enough to catch her breath. "We have to find her!"

Jake moved closer and caught the faint scent of Olivia's perfume. The citrus aroma smelled like freshly cut oranges. He placed his hand gently on her shoulder. "Relax."

"I can't! I got out of the car to let her use the bathroom and she got away from me again. She sprang from my arms before I could put the leash on her." Olivia pushed her hair away from her face. "I've lost her again. Maybe I'm not cut out for this."

"Don't be so hard on yourself. Callie is safe." Jake knew he was wasting his breath. In Olivia's eyes, losing Callie for a second time was unacceptable.

Kyle stepped closer to the adults. "It's okay, Dr. Olivia. Look over there." Kyle grinned and pointed toward Callie, stretched out on the grass, enjoying the warmth of the sun. Kayla had a firm grip on the leash. "Callie is okay."

Olivia ran to the dog and dropped to the ground. She scooped up the animal and snuggled her close against her chest. "I was so worried about you." She kissed the top of Callie's head. "I'm glad you're safe."

Callie returned the affection, licking the side of Olivia's face. It was the first time Jake saw Olivia connect with Callie. This was a good sign. Progress was being made.

Olivia giggled as the dog continued to give

her wet kisses. "This won't happen again. I promise." Olivia placed Callie on the ground and stood to address the class. "I'm sorry if I held everyone up today."

"No harm done." Jake looked out at the group. "Everyone, this is Olivia Hart. She hasn't been a part of our online group, but she'll be joining us. She's my good friend Myrna's granddaughter."

"Hello," the class responded in unison.

Jake clapped his hands. "Is everyone ready to get started?"

"Yes." The group cheered. The outburst caused the dogs to jump to their feet and bark.

"Okay. First, we'll touch a little on your puppy's socialization skills. We want to ensure they become a friendly and confident adult. At home, it's important to introduce your dog to different sounds and to teach them to be okay being alone."

Harry Dearwester, the oldest in the group, raised his hand.

"Yes, Harry. Did you have a question?" Jake asked as the class turned their attention to the portly, gray-haired man.

"Why would we want to teach them how to be alone if they're going to work with people who might have a disability? Shouldn't they learn how to be with other people?" He bent over and patted his eight-week-old retriever, Tex.

"Being comfortable around strangers is a brilliant point, and one I'll touch on in a moment." Jake strolled around the group and eyed each animal. "First, teaching your dog how to remain calm while home alone can help prevent the animal from developing separation anxiety. I can't tell you the number of stories I've heard of dogs becoming destructive when left home alone. Callie is a prime example. Two weeks ago, while the twins were at school, I ran out to the store. Callie appeared to be having a good day, so I let her have the run of the house, rather than crate her."

"Uh-oh," Harry remarked.

"Yes, it was a big mistake. I should have known better. I'll post a couple pictures of the aftermath of tornado Callie on the website."

The group laughed.

"It wasn't a pretty sight, but a prime example of the importance of using a crate early on. That's why purchasing one is at the top of the list of essentials I provided in your welcome packet. I know a couple of you probably already have one. The crate will create a safe place that the dog will want to keep clean. In addition, keeping them in the crate and allowing them out to use the bathroom will teach them that going outside is good."

Jake took notice of Olivia's furrowed brow.

"Is everything okay, Olivia?"

"This just seems so involved. Won't most of this come natural to the dog?"

Being an ER doctor, Olivia knew a lot about human behaviors. Dogs? Not so much. "Has that been your experience so far with Callie?"

Olivia's face reddened. "Not exactly, but I haven't had a lot of time with her."

"These foundational skills need to be taught early on. A good example is the leash."

"I know, I know. Keep it on. I have that rule memorized." Olivia rolled her eyes. "Trust me, I've learned my lesson."

"Do you know why it's so important to keep the animal leashed early in their training?" Jake waited for a response from Olivia, but only received a shrug of her shoulders. "Anyone?" He scanned the group.

A black crow called out overhead.

Jake continued. "It's imperative for your dog to know their limits. Trust me, they will constantly test you. The leash is one way to teach the animal to keep their focus on you, not on their surroundings."

"Like the squirrels running around in the yard," Rebecca called out.

"Exactly. When my dog Tank was a puppy, he tried to go after every squirrel and rabbit that crossed his path. I spent a lot of time chasing him around the ranch. That was a great point, Rebecca," Jake said. "We'll use the leash, along with a dog bed or mat, to teach your puppy the Place command."

George Thielhorn, a middle-aged man who'd recently inherited a nearby ranch from his father, cleared his throat. "What's that?"

By the blank expressions on the faces of the group, except for Rebecca, Jake realized no one was aware of the most essential command to teach your dog. "Some people say it's a magical cue." Jake laughed. "Seriously, though, most new owners think Sit, Stay and Down are the basic training commands to teach. They make the mistake of believing that's all the animal needs to know. But they couldn't be more wrong."

"Yeah, when I first became a Puppy Raiser, my friend told me I was wasting my money on this camp. She said dogs weren't able to learn a bunch of stuff," Rebecca told the group.

"Your friend must not have any experience with service dogs. I'd venture to guess that if she's a dog owner, her dog barks when you ring her doorbell." Jake had a lot of experience with dog owners who believed their animal needed little training.

"She has a Jack Russell. Every time I go to her house, the dog barks nonstop." Rebecca shook her head.

"That's exactly why the Place command is so important. It will teach your dog, in any situation, to settle down onto a dog bed, a blanket or even the dog's favorite place in the house. It will give them a job to do instead of allowing them to choose one for themselves. They might choose jobs like barking at the doorbell, jumping up on people, begging for food at the dinner table, running wild through the house and destroying everything in their path, or jumping out of a car without permission." Jake glanced in Olivia's direction. "These are just a few of the undesirable behaviors of an untrained dog."

George cleared his throat. "If I can teach Maggie this command, I'll be confident with my investment. She's been shredding everything she can get her mouth on. My wife is close to shipping her off to her sister's ranch."

"I don't think that will be necessary, George. Once Maggie learns that Place simply means for her to go to the spot you tell her and stay there until you release her, your wife will be happy. I guarantee it. Maggie will have no choice but to stay. And she'll do it like it's her job, because it is."

"That's a relief," George stated while the rest of the group chatted among themselves.

Olivia remained quiet and attentive. After the way Callie had acted out at Myrna's during

Sunday dinner, Jake was reminded that the dog might need extra attention beyond the camp. At the end of the three-week program, he'd have to evaluate Callie's progress. Either way, he'd made a promise to his friend George. He'd train Callie to assist Myrna, and he planned to keep his word.

"Okay, I'd like for you to pair up and switch dogs with a partner so the animals can get used to being handled by a stranger. We'll circle the ring a few times before you take control of your dog, and then we'll practice a few commands. After that, we'll work a little on your dog's attentiveness by using dog treats to give them a lesson on eye contact. You'll find detailed instructions in the packet I provided. You can practice at home."

Two hours later, the animals and their owners were ready to wrap things up for the evening. While the group said their goodbyes and headed toward their cars, Olivia and Callie lingered behind.

Jake moved toward Olivia, where she sat in the grass, scratching behind Callie's ear. "Did you have a question?" Jake knelt and patted the dog.

Olivia lifted her head and fixed her eyes in his direction. Jake's pulse increased when their fingers brushed.

"I wanted to apologize if I sounded like a know-it-all in class. It's pretty obvious I don't know what I'm doing with Callie."

Olivia stood, and Jake followed her lead.

"There's no need to apologize. You're no different from any other first-time Puppy Raiser I've had in previous camps." Jake doubted his words. Olivia was different. He'd never had to teach someone as beautiful as Olivia, which he had to admit made it difficult to keep his attention on the class. "As I mentioned before, training a dog properly takes a great deal of patience, and trial and error. Keep in mind, Callie is adjusting to her new environment now that she's living at Myrna's house. It's also important to remember that every dog is different. Each will have their own strengths and weaknesses, just like humans."

Olivia nodded. "I see that now. I can't believe how naive I've been to think I could train Callie on my own."

"Well, to quote Myrna, you are a brilliant doctor. It's only natural for you to believe training a dog would come easy to you."

Olivia's face flushed, and she playfully swatted Jake's arm. "Oh, please. I'm far from brilliant." She paused and gazed out over the field. "In fact, lately I've wondered if I'm truly cut out to work in the ER."

"From what I've heard from your grand-mother, I'd say you're probably just exhausted. She's mentioned your long hours."

"I didn't realize how tired I was until I boarded the plane from Miami. The flight attendant had to wake me when we landed." Olivia laughed.

"It sounds like this trip is exactly what you need. I'm sure your husband is missing you, though." Myrna had told Jake about Olivia's husband and his successful career. Maybe that was why he hadn't traveled with her.

"I don't think so. We're divorced." Olivia's face reddened and she avoided eye contact.

"I'm sorry." Jake reached his hand toward her shoulder, but quickly dropped it to his side. "I didn't realize. Myrna never mentioned it." Jake only remembered her talking highly about Ol-ivia's husband. He couldn't deny he was curious as to the reason for their breakup, but it wasn't his place to ask.

"She only learned about it a couple of days ago. I wanted to tell her in person. It's not some-thing I'm proud of."

"I'm sure it's been difficult for you." Jake had a friend who'd gone through a divorce last year. It was tough, especially for his children.

"He didn't want kids." Olivia volunteered the information. She shook her head and looked up at the sky.

Unsure how to respond, Jake remained silent.

"I know what you're thinking. That's something we should have discussed before we got married."

"Didn't you?"

"Many times. In fact, we talked about it early in our relationship. He came from a large family. He told me he wanted a lot of children."

"What changed his mind?" After losing his wife, Jake's children were his world.

Olivia released a sigh and shrugged her shoulders. "He decided he didn't want the responsibility or expense."

Olivia wiped away a stray tear.

"After he told me, he filed for divorce. It all happened so fast, but in retrospect, I wonder if there were signs I had missed. I guess it doesn't matter now. Having kids has been a lifelong dream for me. Maybe he thought he was doing me a favor?"

"You should have children if it's what you want. I couldn't imagine my world without Kyle and Kayla."

A comfortable silence passed before Kyle approached. "Can we take Tank and Callie for a walk?"

Jake glanced at his watch. "I don't think so. You've got math homework to finish before dinner."

"Oh, man." Kyle kicked his tennis shoe into the ground. A cloud of dust erupted.

Jake looked at Olivia. "Math isn't his strongest subject."

"I'm pretty good with it. Maybe I can help," Olivia offered, twisting a strand of her hair.

"That would be awesome!" Kyle bounced on his toes.

"That's kind of you to offer, but I'm sure you have more important things to do."

Olivia shook her head. "Actually, Gammy is having dinner with a friend from church this evening, so I'm on my own."

"Maybe Dr. Olivia can stay and eat with us! Can she, Daddy?"

Jake couldn't help but notice the smile that parted Olivia's lips. Was she open to an invitation to have dinner with his family? Perhaps if she got to know the children better, Olivia might have a more difficult time uprooting her grandmother and taking her away from people who loved her, too. It was worth a try. "We'd love for you to join us. We planned to make homemade pizza, so there will be plenty."

Kayla remained silent. She obviously wasn't as enthused as her brother.

Olivia tilted her head and tucked a strand of hair behind her ear. "I'd love to."

Jake fought to temper the thrill of spending

an evening with Olivia and his children. Knowing now she was single, he had to take a deep breath to wrangle his emotions under control. It wouldn't be wise to go down that road with Olivia. She was only here temporarily. Besides, he was all too familiar with the pain of losing someone you loved. He couldn't take that risk a second time.

Chapter Five

"Do you want me to show you how to roll out the dough, Dr. Olivia?" Kyle offered with a smile. "I had to practice, but I'm pretty good at it now."

An hour after agreeing to come to dinner at Jake's house, Olivia wiped her flour-covered brow with the back of her hand. She always loved to bake, but her ex-husband did most of the cooking, including making pizza from scratch. He considered himself a master chef. Olivia had loved the conversations they shared while he cooked at the beginning of their marriage. She'd sit on the island stool and watch Mark slice and dice. He had the remarkable skill of turning simple ingredients into a mouthwatering meal. But when her schedule at the hospital consumed more of her time, he spent less time in the kitchen and more time at his office.

Olivia took in the spacious kitchen. Apart from the ingredients and bowls strewn across the quartz countertop, the room was immaculate. Except for the kids' drawings on display, the stainless steel appliances sparkled. Olivia would give anything to one day be able to cover her own refrigerator with drawings her children created.

She returned her attention to the task at hand. "This is the most stubborn stuff I've ever seen. I push it forward and it pulls right back." She placed the rolling pin on the counter and kneaded her fingers into the cool dough while appreciating her local pizza shop back home.

Jake laughed and moved toward the roll of paper towels next to the sink. He turned on the faucet and ran the towel twice under the water. While Olivia continued to struggle, he reached across the island. "Here, let me get that." He brushed the dampened paper towel across her forehead. "You had a little flour up there." He pointed to her brow.

His gentle touch ignited warmth in Olivia's cheeks. A moment of awkward silence filled the room.

"Thank you. I guess my secret is out."

"What's that?" Jake asked.

"That I have the local pizza place back home on speed dial."

Jake grinned. "I didn't want to say anything, but that dough has had you tangled up for quite a while. Don't be so hard on yourself. I probably should have kept the dough at room temperature for a while longer. Would you like a hand?"

Olivia pulled away and rotated her palms face up. "Yours are probably cleaner than mine." Sticky clumps of dough clung to her fingertips.

Kyle clattered around in a nearby drawer and pulled out another sparkling rolling pin. "My mommy taught me and Daddy all the secrets to make a pizza. It's pretty easy once you get the hang of it."

Callie and Tank both barked in the backyard.

"I thought Kayla was going to feed the dogs?" Jake looked down at Kyle.

"She said she was." Kyle shrugged his shoulder.

The barking continued, but this time, it was only Callie. Olivia walked to the sink, rinsed her hands and peered out the window above the faucet. Tank was curled up underneath the weeping willow while Callie ran circles around the yard. Kayla was nowhere in sight. "Do you mind if I go check on Callie?" She reached for the hand towel and then turned to Jake.

"Do you want me to go with you?" Kyle volunteered. His eyelashes fluttered.

Olivia smiled. Kyle was such a thoughtful little boy. Thoughts swirled in her mind. He was exactly the type of child she dreamed of having one day. "Maybe you should stay here and help your daddy with the pizza. The two of you are much better at handling the dough than I am."

"Okay, but what toppings do you want? I hope not those fishy things." Kyle crinkled his nose.

Olivia knelt in front of Kyle. "No way. I love cheese. In fact, I've never met a cheese I didn't like."

The corners of Kyle's mouth tilted up into a smile. "Me too!" He jumped up and down.

"What about the pepperoni lovers over here?" Jake waved his arms.

Kyle rolled his eyes. "My daddy and Kayla love pepperoni."

Olivia stood and gazed down at Kyle. "Let me go outside and get Callie settled. I'll ask Kayla if she wants to help. The two pepperoni fans can make their pizza and we'll make ours. How does that sound?"

"Awesome! After dinner, can we do the jigsaw puzzle in the dining room? It's got tons of cool farm animals." Kyle's smile lit up his face.

Jake placed his hand on his son's shoulder. "That will have to wait. Remember, you have math homework to do."

Kyle's smile faded, but quickly returned when

he looked up at Olivia. "But you're going to help me, right?"

"Of course. Earlier, I said I would help you. I always keep my word." Olivia understood the importance of keeping her word, especially to a child. After her father died and her mother began to abuse alcohol, broken promises were ubiquitous.

"Some grown-ups don't, so I was just checking." Kyle returned his focus back to the dough. "I won't touch it until you come back. Daddy told me that Mommy always said don't work the dough too much because it will fight back."

"I think she was right. I'll be back." Olivia headed to the back door.

Outside, Olivia's steps slowed. She admired the bright yellows and reds of the snapdragons lining the backside of the privacy fence. Their sweet fragrance drifted through the late-spring air. Unable to recall the last time she'd slowed long enough to notice flowers, she wondered when the season had changed. Living in Miami was a never-ending race from the moment her feet hit the floor each morning. As she studied the flower bed, she wondered if Jake's wife had created the garden or if the family had planted the flowers together. The latter was a beautiful image. Something she'd often dreamed of doing one day with her family.

Callie raced toward Olivia, pulling her mind back to the moment. She reached down and pulled the dog into her arms. "Hey, girl. What's got you so riled up?" Callie licked the side of her face. "You want some attention? Is that it?"

Olivia scanned the yard, but there was no sign of Kayla. A hint of a breeze cooled her face. On the opposite side of the grounds, she spied a small house with light pink shutters and a lime-green roof. It looked like the playhouse her best friend had when they were in grade school. Kayla had to be inside.

With Callie still in her arms, Olivia advanced across the grass, careful not to frighten the child if she was inside. The door to the house was ajar. Olivia peeked through the crack. White twinkle lights lined the ceiling. Her heart squeezed at the sight of Kayla sitting on the floor with a picture frame in her hands and tears racing down her cheeks.

Olivia's first instinct was to retreat. Go back into the house and pretend she hadn't seen Kayla. But how could she? Kayla was obviously upset. If Olivia entered the house uninvited, she could make matters worse. Kayla had made her feelings toward her apparent.

Olivia contemplated her next move. During her career, she'd treated plenty of children in the ER. What if she couldn't help Kayla? But what if she could? She straightened her shoulders, raised her hand and gently knocked on the pink wooden door. "Kayla, may I come inside?"

A bumblebee buzzed past while Olivia waited for an answer that never came. She took a deep breath, reached out and tightened her grip on the doorknob. She opened the door and stepped inside. To her surprise, despite the small outer appearance of the house, once inside Olivia didn't have to hunch or lower her head. It was spacious enough for two people. "Are you okay, sweetie?" Olivia froze. With closer proximity, she could see the picture of a strikingly beautiful pregnant woman contained inside the frame. The woman had brown hair that cascaded well past her shoulders.

Tears streamed down Kayla's face.

Olivia took a deep breath, trying to compose herself. Her first instinct was to drop to the ground and wrap her arms around Kayla. She'd tell her that the pain wouldn't last forever, but Olivia knew that wouldn't be the truth. The ache of losing her father still clung to her like a weighted vest. Losing a parent was something a child should never have to experience, but the stark reality was she and Kayla shared the same heartache. Olivia remained quiet, allowing Kayla time to respond to her uninvited guest.

Callie wiggled and whimpered in Olivia's

arms. She placed her down and Callie's toenails scratched the wooden floor as she ran to Kayla. The dog pounced on her lap and licked her hands that were still clutching the frame.

Next, Callie slid her tongue along the child's face. A slight giggle erupted from Kayla's lips.

"Okay, Callie." Olivia patted her hand against her leg to get the dog's attention. "That's enough."

"She hasn't learned her place yet," Kayla whispered.

Olivia stared at Kayla for a moment before realizing what she was referring to. "You're right. Once she learns her place, when I put her on the ground, she'll stay, right?"

Kayla nodded and wiped her cheek. "Yeah."

Olivia knelt to face Kayla. "Is it okay if I sit with you?"

Kayla gave a slight shoulder shrug. Olivia took it as a yes.

Positioned on the floor, Olivia pulled her knees against her chest, looked around the room and sighed. "When I was your age, my friend had a clubhouse just like this, except it didn't have electricity. I always wanted one of my own."

Callie finally settled down on the floor and rested her head against Kayla's leg.

"My daddy built it for me." Kayla scratched the top of Callie's head.

"That was nice of him." Olivia took in the space. She admired the pink lace curtains covering the two windows. A table with two chairs sat on top of a thick pink throw rug. Kayla was certainly daddy's little girl. "It feels so cozy."

Kayla looked down at the photograph and ran her fingers across the glass. "He made it after my mommy died."

At a loss for words, Olivia remained silent.

"He thought I might want it to get away from the boys in the house." Kayla kept her eyes fixed on the photo. "But I think he didn't want to think about Mommy."

A lump formed in Olivia's throat. It was a wise observation for a six-year-old. Olivia could remember her mother responding the same way after losing her husband. The day after the funeral, Olivia's mother decided she wanted to repaint the interior walls of the entire house. Day after day, her mother went nonstop, never sleeping or taking time to eat, which meant she didn't prepare any meals. Olivia ate cereal for breakfast, lunch and dinner until the milk ran out. Then she ate the cereal dry. It wasn't until Gammy and Pops moved in that she finally had some normalcy.

"Do you mind?" Olivia reached for the photograph.

Kayla clung to the frame for a moment and

then finally let go. She handed it to Olivia. Her eyes never left the photograph.

"Your mother was beautiful." Olivia studied the woman who looked so much like her children. Her brown eyes sparkled with glints of gold. Her skin was like that of a porcelain doll. "What's the best thing you remember about her?"

Kayla's eyes widened. She bit her lower lip and shook her head.

Olivia passed the picture back to Kayla. "You know, it's okay to talk about your mommy."

Her brow crinkled. "It is?"

"Yes, that's how we can hold tight to the memories. I know that's what your mommy would want."

"Every time I try to tell a story about her, my daddy and Kyle talk about something else. Kyle says it hurts Daddy too much. He says we shouldn't mention Mommy. But I'm afraid if I don't, I'm going to forget her."

Olivia gazed around the space before meeting Kayla's eyes. "Well, right now it's just me and you. I'd love to hear a story about your mommy."

"Really?"

Olivia nodded.

Kayla inched closer to Olivia and smiled. "My mommy loved snow. We used to make giant snowmen in front of the house and dress them in Daddy's clothes." She giggled.

Olivia pictured the scene in her mind and her heart warmed. "That sounds like fun."

"Yeah. She made everything fun. After, we'd come inside and have cocoa and warm brownies with strawberry Jell-O."

"Tell me more," Olivia encouraged Kayla.

"Before school, on days when it was cold, my mommy would put my coat, hat and gloves over the heat vent on the kitchen floor. Everything was warm and toasty when I got ready to catch the bus."

"I'm sure it felt nice." It sounded like something Olivia's father would have done for her. He was always doting on her.

Kayla looked up with tears in her eyes. "I really miss her."

For a second, Olivia hesitated, but when Kayla leaned into her arms, Olivia provided an embrace. She stroked the back of Kayla's head and held her tight. Her hair smelled like sweet honeysuckle. "I know you do, sweetie."

"It's not fair. All my friends have mommies. They get to do fun stuff together like me and my mommy used to do."

"I'm sure that's hard." Olivia kissed the top of her head.

Kayla pulled back and looked up. "I'm sorry

I was mean to you when you lost Callie." Kayla blinked several times.

Olivia laughed. "You were just being protective."

"My daddy was right."

"About what?"

"He says sometimes my mouth speaks before my head has time to think."

"I used to do the same when I was your age." Olivia recalled many times that her mouth got her into trouble. "You know, you and I have a lot in common."

"Like what? I'm not as pretty as you. I'd like to be a doctor one day, but I'm not smart like you."

Kayla's lack of confidence was unsettling. "You're a beautiful young lady. Don't compare yourself to anyone else. God made you exactly how He wanted you to be. Did you know there is no other person in the world with the same fingerprints as you?"

Kayla looked down and examined her fingers. "Really? That's cool."

"I hope you'll always remember that you can do anything you put your mind to. If you want to be a doctor, then work hard in school and you'll reach your goal." Olivia placed her hand underneath Kayla's chin, tipping it upward. "Sweetie, don't let anyone steal your dreams."

Kayla nodded. "Okay. I promise." She bit her lower lip. "So, what do we have in common?"

Outside, a woodpecker drilled the side of the clubhouse as daylight faded.

"When I was a little older than you are right now, my daddy died."

"He did?" Her brow crinkled. "I'm really sorry."

"Thank you." The years had passed, but the pain was like a wound that kept getting bumped and never healed. If Olivia closed her eyes, she could picture her father lying on the kitchen floor. She had opened her mouth to scream, but there was no sound. Dropping to the floor, she'd rested her head against her father's chest and cried. "The kids at school never seemed to understand. Sure, they were nice and apologetic at first, but as time passed, they seemed to forget about it, but I never could."

Kayla's head quickly bobbed up and down. "That's exactly how I feel."

"It's important to remember that your friends aren't doing it on purpose. They've just never been in your shoes. It's like being in a private club. Only the members truly know what's going on."

Olivia wasn't sure if this made sense to Kayla. Even as an adult, it was difficult for her to understand why God would allow a child to lose a parent. She thought of Jake and his loss. How did anyone move past such a heartbreaking event?

Kayla pushed her hair away from her face. "I sure wish I wasn't a member of this club. I don't like to feel this way."

"Even though it doesn't seem like it, you can always talk to your daddy or Kyle." After Olivia's father passed, without siblings, it wasn't until Gammy came to live with them that Olivia had someone to reminisce with about her mother.

"But I don't want to make my daddy sad. I can see the look on his face when I mention Mommy. And Kyle seems like he's already forgotten about her."

"People grieve a loss in different ways, sweetie. It might be too painful for your father and brother to talk about her."

"But I'm afraid we're going to all forget. I always feel better after I talk about her. Sometimes I even tell my stuffed animals stories about her."

"I did the same thing." Olivia paused. "I have an idea. Maybe while I'm here, you can talk to me about your mommy and I'll talk to you about my father. Does that sound like a good idea?"

Kayla lunged forward and wrapped her arms around Olivia's neck. Warmth surged through

Olivia's body. She'd never held a child in this way. It felt good—too good. Getting attached wasn't part of her plan. She was here to help her gammy and convince her she'd be better off in Florida. Olivia would never be happy living in a small town. Yet the feeling she had with Kayla in her arms seemed to bring her more happiness than she'd felt in years.

Jake rubbed his eyes and did a double take. Were his eyes playing tricks on him? He blinked three times and once again looked through the kitchen window. He wasn't mistaken. Olivia and Kayla were walking through the backyard holding hands. After Olivia's arrival, Kayla avoided interaction with her, but now they looked like best friends. Kayla and Olivia becoming buddies wasn't good. Kayla's heart could break if this new friendship continued to blossom. Olivia's time in Bluebell was temporary.

"Wash your hands, sweetie," Olivia instructed Kayla as they stepped into the kitchen.

"Okay." Without hesitation, Kayla skipped to the sink, humming a tune.

"Do you want to help me make our pizza?" Jake asked Kayla as he drizzled olive oil on the dough.

Kyle glanced up from the counter. "Yeah, Kay. You help Daddy. Me and Dr. Olivia are making this pizza." He motioned with his hand across the ingredients. "See all the extra cheese? This is ours."

"I want to work with Dr. Olivia," Kayla said. "After dinner, she's going to help me with my book report."

It wasn't his imagination. Something had occurred outside between Olivia and Kayla. But what?

"I thought Dr. Olivia was going to help me with my math after?" Kyle kicked his shoe against the wood floor.

Jake and Olivia looked at each other. Her brow arched while she appeared to wait for him to resolve the dispute.

"Dr. Olivia offered to help your brother with his math first. You know he's been struggling."

Olivia cleared her throat. "Maybe, if it's okay with you, I can help both of them."

"That's kind of you to offer to help Kayla too, but I'm sure you'll want to get home after we have our pizza." Jake assumed Olivia was being nice, so he offered a way out.

"I'd love to help. I'd just be going home to an empty house. Gammy said not to expect her until at least ten o'clock." Olivia pinched a mound of cheese and sprinkled it over the pizza. "I offered to drive her, but she said she'd be fine. With her poor vision, I worry about her being on the road after dark, so it might be best for me to stay and keep myself busy. I'll just sit up worrying otherwise."

Jake nodded. "She can be as stubborn as a rusty bolt."

Olivia chuckled. "I think you're right. She probably shouldn't be driving day or night. I need to find out when she last had her license renewed."

Jake agreed. He also worried about Myrna being out on the road, particularly at night. But taking away someone's driving privileges was a sensitive topic. It would be best for a medical professional or someone at the DMV to handle it. "I believe Myrna renewed last summer, but it appears her eyes have deteriorated since then."

"Quit touching the dough, Kyle. You're going to ruin it." Kayla interrupted the adults, bringing them back to the task at hand.

"All right, I think it's time to get these pizzas into the oven. Kyle, do you want to help me with the pepperoni? We don't want to keep Dr. Olivia out too late."

Kyle jumped off the step stool and sped to his father's side. He snatched a piece of pepperoni and popped it into his mouth.

"I said help, not eat." Jake ruffled the top of his son's hair.

Kyle giggled, and the oven beeped.

"Ours is ready to go in," Olivia announced.

"Great. The pot holders are in the top drawer to the right of the oven." Jake placed the last sprinkle of garlic powder over the pizza.

Olivia's eyes popped as she peered inside the oversize oven. "The oven is huge. We can put the pizzas side by side."

"Daddy bought the oven for Mommy. She loved to cook. He said one Thanksgiving she baked three turkeys at once for the homeless shelter in Denver." Kayla spoke with pride.

Kyle nudged his sister in the arm.

"What?" Kayla flinched.

"It makes Daddy sad when we talk about Mommy."

"But Dr. Olivia told me it's okay. She said it's good to remember. It's what Mommy would want." Kayla shot a look in Olivia's direction.

Olivia's eyes shifted to Jake.

Jake cleared his throat. He couldn't miss the redness in Olivia's face. "Dr. Olivia is right. We should never forget your mommy."

"Then how come you don't like us to talk about her?" Kayla wrapped her arms around her stomach.

It was true. When his children or someone from town mentioned Laura, he did his best to change the subject. Despite the advice from Pastor Kidd, Jake struggled to keep her memory alive. It was too painful. It wasn't fair to Kayla and Kyle. He prayed about it every morning. "I believed not talking about your mommy protected you, but really, I wasn't giving you the opportunity to grieve the loss of your mother in your own way. It was easier for me not to talk about what had happened. I've been wrong. I'm sorry."

Kayla moved toward Jake and wrapped her arms around his waist. "It's okay, Daddy. I don't want you to be sad. When I was outside, I told Dr. Olivia stories about Mommy, and it made me feel good. Maybe you should try it, too."

Jake's heart warmed. "I think that's the best idea I've heard in a long time."

Kayla's smile lit up her face. "You do?"

"Yes. In fact, I think I have the perfect way to share your stories about your mother."

Kyle and Kayla moved closer to Jake. Their eyes grew wide. "How?" they both asked.

"Maybe each night before we say our bedtime prayers, you can take turns sharing something you remember about your mommy."

"We can talk about Mommy?" Kayla questioned as though she were asking for the impossible.

Jake nodded. "If you'd like, we can start tonight."

"Yes!" Kyle did a fist pump. "I can't wait to go to bed!"

The adults laughed.

"But what about you, Daddy?"

Jake looked down at Kayla.

"You knew Mommy a lot longer than we did. You must have tons of stories. Can you share, too?"

Jake's heart squeezed. *God, give me the strength.* "There's nothing I'd rather do more." He'd known Laura since college, so there'd be an endless amount of stories to share with Kyle and Kayla. He'd do his best to remember every detail about his wife. In his desire to protect his children, he'd actually done more harm than good. But thanks to Olivia, that was all about to change. He glanced in her direction and she smiled. A twinge of excitement coursed through him, but he quickly pushed it away. He had to remain loyal to Laura's memory.

Chapter Six

Late Friday afternoon the sun dipped behind the Rockies, prompting Olivia to check her watch for the third time in twenty minutes.

"Come, Callie." She clapped her hands three times, and the puppy obeyed the command. "Good girl. Let's head inside and get your dinner." Since returning from Camp Bow Wow, Olivia had worked on the homework Jake had assigned at the end of their session. Callie was making good progress, but according to Jake, she still had a lot to learn. Olivia couldn't deny the idea of spending more time with Jake was appealing. He was easy on the eyes, but she needed to remind herself this trip was for Gammy, not to fall for a handsome service dog trainer and his adorable children.

Noting the time, Olivia shivered. It would be dark soon, but Gammy was still out. When

Olivia had arrived home from camp, a scribbled note was on the kitchen table. Gammy had taken Ruth Westerly for a medical procedure after her ride had fallen through. Olivia admired her grandmother's generous heart, but the idea of her driving home in the dark didn't sit well. She didn't have a phone number to call Ruth to check if Gammy had dropped her off. She'd have to try her grandmother's cell for the second time.

Olivia stepped inside the laundry room. Callie jumped up and pawed at Olivia's feet. "I know you're hungry. Just give me a minute." Callie released a bark, followed by a whimper.

Olivia removed the sealed canister of dry food from the shelf and poured it into Callie's dish. The ravenous pup pushed her face into the bowl and gulped the meal. "I guess Jake was right when he said puppies have enormous appetites. All that exercise at camp made you hungry. Didn't it, girl?" Olivia scratched the top of the animal's head. "Eat your dinner. I'm going to fix something for me and Gammy. I'm starving, too."

Outside, thunder rumbled in the distance. Olivia scanned the contents of the refrigerator as she rubbed the back of her neck. A flash of lightning filled the kitchen at the same time as her phone sounded an alarm. Olivia dropped the head of lettuce she'd pulled from the shelf.

A tornado watch has been issued in your area.

What? Living in Florida, Olivia was used to the occasional tornado warning, but even living in Colorado as a child, she'd never realized the state experienced these weather patterns, too. Or maybe she didn't pay much attention to the weather as a child. Her heart hammered against her chest. She snatched the phone off the countertop to check the radar. Two quick taps on the screen caused her hands to shake. A huge red blob covered the map. Severe weather was heading toward Denver and it appeared to be moving toward Bluebell Canyon.

Olivia quickly pulled up her contact list and smashed her finger on Gammy's name. Again, the call went straight to voice mail, but this time Olivia left a message. "Gammy, please call me as soon as you hear this. There's a severe storm coming. Wherever you are, wait for me. I can come pick you up. Please call me." She pressed End and slipped the device into her back pocket. An engine rumbled outside. Was Gammy finally home? She raced to the front window and peeked through the slats of the plantation shutters. A delivery truck was in the driveway. A man stepped from the vehicle and climbed the front steps carrying a large box. Before he rang the bell, Olivia flung open the door to greet him.

"I have a package for Mrs. Hart." He peeked around Olivia's shoulder. "Is she home?"

Olivia accepted the delivery. "Thank you." She turned and placed the box on the chair inside the foyer. "No, she's not here right now, but I'll be sure she gets the package."

"I wanted to thank her for the cookies she baked for me last week. They were the best I've ever had. She's okay, isn't she?"

The young man's genuine concern touched Olivia. This would only happen in a small town like Bluebell. "She's fine, thank you. She drove a friend to a medical appointment."

"It must be Mrs. Westerly. She had her colonoscopy scheduled for today. I would have driven her, but I couldn't get the time off from work." His brow knit. "I hope Mrs. Hart gets home before the storm hits. The radio says it could be a big one."

The pulse in Olivia's neck fluttered. "I hope so, too. I'll let her know you enjoyed the cookies." Olivia glanced at the name tag pinned to his company shirt.

"You be safe too, Jeff."

Olivia closed the door and considered her next move. Jake. He would have a phone number for Ruth. Actually, she should have asked Jeff. He probably had the entire town on his phone.

Olivia slipped her phone from her pocket and intently scrolled her contact list. When Jake's number appeared, she tapped to call. Her fingers tightened against the phone. He answered on the first ring.

"Hey, Olivia. What's up?"

"I'm sorry to bother you. It's Gammy." Her voice shook. "She's not home and there's a storm coming. I'm worried."

"I'll be right over."

The last thing Olivia wanted to do was disrupt his evening with the children, especially if it was a false alarm and her grandmother walked through the door any minute. "I don't want to trouble you. I wanted to know if you had a telephone number for Ruth Westerly?" Olivia explained the situation.

"I'll call Ruth and call you back." Jake quickly ended the call.

Olivia paced the floor and prayed her grandmother was safe. Maybe it was only a poor cell signal. But something gnawed at her, telling her otherwise.

Olivia's phone gave a half ring before she answered Jake's call. "Did you reach Ruth?"

"There was no answer. But I'm not surprised.

Ruth lives alone. Her husband passed away a few years ago."

Olivia sensed the concerned tone in Jake's voice. "What should I do? I don't have a good feeling about this. Gammy should be home by now. The weather report mentioned tornadoes."

"Stay put. I'll be right over." Jake hung up.

Despite the situation, knowing Jake was coming over instilled a sense of comfort in Olivia. Something she hadn't felt since before the dissolution of her marriage.

Less than fifteen minutes later, she heard the crunching of tires on gravel out front.

Callie jumped to attention and raced to the door. Olivia followed.

Before Jake knocked, Olivia flung it open.

"It's raining," he announced as he wiped his feet on the welcome mat and stepped inside.

"Where are the children?" Olivia asked.

"I dropped them off at my brother's house. I didn't want them to worry when it turns out to be nothing."

Olivia admired Jake. He always put his children first and would do whatever he could to protect them. "Good thinking."

"You mentioned a medical appointment. Do you know what time?"

Olivia nodded. "Her note said it was three o'clock."

Jake rubbed his hand across his chin. "Anything else?"

"No."

Jake walked across the floor, then pivoted. "I can try to call Dr. Dickerson. He's the town doctor. Most likely, he referred Ruth to a doctor in Denver, or perhaps he set up the medical procedure."

"That's a great idea."

"Don't get too excited. I'm not sure how much Dr. Dickerson can share, given the confidentiality laws." Jake pulled his phone from his back pocket and tapped the screen.

Olivia's shoulders sank. Jake was right. She should have asked Jeff the delivery boy since he knew about Ruth's appointment.

Jake looked up from his device. "I'm not getting a good signal in here—could be the storm. Do you mind if I go out on the porch to make the call?"

Heavy rain pelted the roof. Water overflowed from the gutter.

"Of course not." Olivia appreciated Jake asking permission. She wondered if Jake realized how much she loved her grandmother. Her thoughts quickly returned to Gammy being out on the road in these treacherous conditions. Why didn't she push the issue more? Olivia should have tried harder to convince her grandmother that with her vision deteriorating, it was too dangerous to drive—particularly after dark.

Jake stepped back inside the house. His face was wet from the driving rain.

"Did you find out anything about the doctor? We need to find her!"

Jake approached and gently placed his hands on her upper arms. His stormy eyes connected with hers, creating another wave of nausea, along with a swarm of butterflies. "Please, try to calm down. Dr. Dickerson said he referred Ruth to a gastrointestinal doctor in Denver. Ruth had told him her appointment was at one. He's calling the doctor's office now to find out what time they left his office. He said he'd call right back."

Olivia inhaled a deep breath and released it.

"If Ruth's procedure was on time, they should have been on the road long before four o'clock." Jake glanced at his watch. "It's after six now. They should be home any minute."

Outside, a gust of wind rattled the shutters before tapping sounded against the windows.

Jake turned at the noise. "That sounds like hail." He walked toward the window and opened the plantation shutter. "I think small pellets are falling. It looks like the winds are picking up, too. Make sure you have a full charge on your phone in case we lose power."

Olivia hurried into the kitchen and retrieved her charger from her purse. She plugged the phone into the outlet, keeping the phone turned on so she wouldn't miss a call. A chill raced up her spine thinking about Gammy in the storm.

Jake stepped into the kitchen and his cell phone rang. He answered on the first ring. Olivia heard a voice on the other end. Thankfully the connection was better. She busied her hands by dumping the cold pot of coffee from earlier in the day into the sink and sent up a silent prayer for her grandmother.

Jake pocketed his cell and approached Olivia. "What did Dr. Dickerson say?"

"It looks like we'll be making a road trip. Dr. Dickerson spoke with the physician who performed the colonoscopy. He'd had an earlier cancellation, so he actually finished up with Ruth around three fifteen."

The sudden turn of events was unsettling. She had hoped her grandmother's absence was because of the doctor running behind schedule, but Jake just confirmed that the opposite was true. Olivia ran her fingers through her hair. "Then why hasn't Gammy dropped off Ruth? Something isn't right." A sudden beeping from her phone made her jump.

A severe thunderstorm warning has been issued in your area.

Olivia read the message and shuddered.

"I'm going to put a call in to my friend. He's a state trooper in Denver. Maybe he can tell us of any accident reported." Jake drew his phone from his pocket.

Olivia could barely breathe. If anything happened to Gammy, she would be all alone in the world. "We have to go find her," Olivia pleaded with Jake while he searched his device for his friend's number.

She paced the kitchen floor. Callie nipped at her heels while Jake spoke on the phone.

Minutes later, he ended the call and approached Olivia.

"Has he heard of any accidents?" Olivia wrapped her arms tight around her waist.

Jake's expression was solemn. "My buddy Nick isn't on duty, but I spoke with Dispatch. They don't have any accident reported along the route Myrna would have been traveling."

Olivia dropped her arms to her sides and grabbed her purse off the counter. She unplugged her phone from the charger and tossed it inside her bag. "I need to go find her."

Callie barked twice.

"I can't sit here waiting." She bit her lower lip. The tears she'd fought to hold back broke free and streamed down her cheeks. "My grandmother is all I have."

Jake moved closer and pulled her into his arms. "Please don't cry. She'll be okay. We'll find her. I promise."

For a moment, Olivia found comfort in Jake's warm embrace, but that was a dangerous place to be. She quickly pulled away, turned toward the window and the pounding rain, and shivered. "Let's go find my gammy."

Minutes later, they were on the road. Jake gripped the steering wheel and willed the windshield wipers to move faster. The heavy rain was blinding. The car's high beams did little to assist Jake with the poor visibility.

Despite his cautious speed, he suddenly lost control of the car.

With the treacherous weather, Jake would have preferred to make this trip alone, but he couldn't blame Olivia for wanting to help with the search. She loved her grandmother and was concerned for her safety.

Olivia leaned forward with a paper towel in hand, frantically wiping the fog that the defroster failed to eliminate. "Can you see?" Her voice shook as she leaned closer to him.

Their shoulders brushed, providing a moment of comfort despite the weather conditions. Jake shook off the feeling. He needed to keep his focus off Olivia and on the road. This was another reason he'd wanted to search for Myrna on his own. Lately, Olivia's presence made him feel like a nervous schoolboy.

"Do you think it would be better if we use the main interstate to get to Denver? These country roads have huge potholes. I don't think Gammy would go this way." Olivia continued her attempt to clear the windshield, which seemed to be a losing battle.

"You're right about the highway being a safer route, but Myrna won't travel on the interstate. She always avoids the highway and takes the back roads because she doesn't like to drive over forty miles per hour."

Olivia tore another towel from the roll. "I guess her eyes are worse than she wants any of us to know."

"Long before Myrna's diagnosis, she wouldn't get on the interstate. She said merging into fast-moving traffic caused her blood pressure to sky-rocket." Jake laughed.

Olivia leaned back against the leather seat. "It sounds like you know my grandmother better than I do. It's kind of sad, don't you think?"

"Don't be so hard on yourself. It happens. Things aren't like they used to be."

"How so?"

Jake eased his foot from the accelerator as the car rounded a sharp curve. A flash of lightning lit up the sky. "Families used to live closer to one another. They were there to help each other during times of need."

"From what I hear, you still honor that tradition. Gammy told me you and your family all live on the same plot of land. She also shared how you and your brothers worked together to help your father care for your mother before she went into the nursing home." Olivia paused and released a sigh. "It must be a comfort to know there's always someone around who has your back."

"Yeah, it's nice to have family nearby, but it doesn't take blood to make a family. Your grandmother is proof of that. Of course, my brothers always come through for me, but your grandmother was my rock after my wife died. She helped me and the kids so much in those first few months. I'm not sure I would have survived without her."

Olivia squirmed in her seat. She wrapped her arms around her stomach. "I'm glad she was there to help you. She did the same for me after my father died. Once my mother turned to drinking as a coping mechanism, I had no one to help me deal with the loss. I honestly can't fathom what would have become of my life if Gammy hadn't come to take care of me. I hope you can understand why it's important for me to bring her back to Miami. I want to help her like she helped me. With her eyes getting worse, she can't continue to live alone, with or without a guide dog. Tonight is a perfect example. Callie wouldn't have stopped Gammy from driving her friend to Denver, but I could have."

"I don't want to argue with you about moving Myrna. We both want what's best for her. I agree she shouldn't have made this long drive, but I think her heart overpowered her logic." Now wasn't the time to debate the moving issue. Jake knew plenty of disabled people who lived independently with the help of a service dog and upgrades to their home.

They rode in silence for the next few miles. Olivia continued with her attempts to reach Myrna, but the calls went straight to voice mail.

"Look! Do you see those lights flashing ahead?" Olivia pointed.

Jake slowed as the wipers continued at a rapid pace, trying desperately to keep up with the deluge. "That's the driveway to the Potters' farm. It's been empty since Sam died over a year ago. They have everything tied up in probate court."

"There was a car. I saw it. Pull over!"

Jake hit the turn signal and navigated his extended-cab truck off the road. The headlights hit the familiar white sedan and his pulse slowed. "That's Myrna's car."

"Thank You, God!" Olivia cried out. "I hope they're okay."

Jake placed the car into Park and turned off the engine. "You wait here. I'll go check on them." He unfastened his seat belt, pulled the hood of his jacket over his head and opened the door.

"Not on your life." Olivia repeated Jake's actions. "I'm going, too." She jumped from the car.

Jake jogged to Myrna's vehicle with Olivia close behind and tapped on the driver's-side window. He didn't want to frighten the women. With the rain coming down so hard, it was likely they couldn't see him and Olivia.

A second later, the window rolled down about half an inch. "I've been praying that you would come," Myrna said.

"Why didn't you call? Are you two okay?" Jake scanned Myrna's face. His shoulders relaxed when he saw no sign of distress.

"When the weather got bad, I pulled over at the first safe spot. I tried to call, but my cell phone battery went dead."

Olivia peered into the back seat. "Is Ruth okay?"

Jake looked through the glass. He spotted Ruth stretched out across the back seat with a yellow afghan covering her.

"She fell asleep ten minutes outside of Denver. I guess the anesthesia is still working on her." Myrna glanced over her shoulder at her friend. "Poor thing. On our way out of the doctor's office, she said she was starving after fasting. She wanted a double cheeseburger. Then, within seconds of getting into the car, she was out."

"I wish you would have used Ruth's phone to call. I've been worried sick." Olivia sighed.

Myrna unbuckled her seat belt. "Ruth doesn't have a cell phone. I gave her one last year for Christmas, but she donated it to Penny, who runs the women's shelter in Smithville. She said Penny could use it more than her."

Olivia frowned. "With your eyes, you shouldn't drive without a fully charged phone. In fact, you shouldn't drive, period. What if we hadn't found you?"

Myrna pulled her hood over her head. "Maybe we should wait and discuss my driving privileges when we're all safely home."

"Okay, ladies, we'll talk about this later. Olivia, you can follow me. We'll swing by Ruth's house and drop her off first."

Olivia nodded.

Jake helped Myrna from the car and circled her around to the passenger side while Olivia took the driver's seat.

With the women safely inside the car, Jake

trudged across the muddy driveway to his truck. Based on their earlier conversation, it was clear Olivia still believed Myrna would be better off in Florida. However, the more he learned about Olivia's past, he was gaining a better understanding of Olivia's position. She loved Myrna as much as he and his children did. Of course, protecting Kyle and Kayla from any additional pain and suffering was his number one priority. He'd have to continue with the upgrades on Myrna's home and pray Olivia would reconsider her plan. Bluebell would not be the same without Myrna Hart…or without the woman who was slowly stealing his heart.

Chapter Seven

Olivia used the back of her palm to wipe the moisture from her cheek. She tugged the cool satin sheet under her chin and squeezed her eyes closed. A soft whimper filled the guest room, followed by another round of wetness across her eyebrows. She slowly opened one eye and found herself face-to-face with a shiny brown nose.

"What are you doing up so early, Callie?"

The puppy dug her paws furiously into the fluffy down comforter and barked.

Olivia eyed the digital clock on the dresser and jerked her head off her pillow.

Eleven fifteen.

Kicking the covers tangled around her ankles, she sprang from the bed. When her bare feet hit the floor, she nearly tripped.

Callie barked and raced to the door.

Jake had stressed the importance of keeping

Callie on a schedule. Last night, before going to bed, she'd double-checked the alarm on her phone. Had she been so tired that she slept through it?

Olivia sprinted to the closet and quickly dressed. The shower could wait until after she took Callie for a walk and fed her breakfast.

"Come on, girl." Olivia opened the bedroom door and raced for the staircase. Halfway down, her socked feet skidded to a stop.

"Whoa!"

Olivia stopped just short of running full force into Jake, who was hunched over on the landing.

"Where's the fire?" Clutching a piece of carpet in his right hand, Jake pushed himself up. His biceps bulged through his Beckett's Canine Training T-shirt.

Olivia's messy hair and flannel lounge pants were proof that the last person she had expected to see this morning was Jake. Had she known he was in the house, she would have at least run a comb through the tangled mane.

"I overslept." Olivia glanced down at Callie. Warmth filled her cheeks. "I never oversleep. The day is half-gone! I should have taken Callie out hours ago. I marked my calendar for a two-hour hike this morning."

"Relax. Not everything in life needs to be planned. You must have needed the sleep, and it's hard to resist the positive effects of the mountain air." Jake winked. "Don't worry. Myrna took Callie out before she left."

Guilt took hold. First, Callie ran off on her watch, not once, but twice. Now Olivia got caught slacking off on her puppy-raising duties.

She twisted a strand of hair. "I'm sorry. We'll get out of your way." Olivia called to Callie. "Come on, girl. Let's get your breakfast before it's lunchtime."

"Myrna fed her already. I think she got up with the chickens." Jake laughed.

If Olivia wanted to keep up with her grandmother, she'd have to get a louder alarm clock. "Where did Gammy go?" Getting her grandmother to sit still long enough to talk to her about relinquishing her driver's license and relying more on neighbors for transportation would be a challenge. Following yesterday's scare, Olivia was more convinced that driving was no longer safe for Gammy.

"She's working her volunteer shift at the library from eight until noon. Then she was meeting Hilde for lunch in Denver. They also planned to do some shopping for the twins' birthday party."

"Boy, I hope I have that kind of energy when I'm her age. Gammy has a way of making me look like a lazy bum."

Jake laughed. "She doesn't allow a blade of grass to grow under her feet. She loves to do for others."

Since arriving in Bluebell, Olivia kept witnessing the positive impact her grandmother had on her community. "When is the twins' party?"

"It's a week from today. I still can't believe they're going to be seven years old." Jake shook his head. "You're invited, of course."

"That's nice of you. It sounds like fun." Olivia admired Jake. Raising his children without their mother couldn't be easy, yet he seemed to handle things effortlessly.

"I'll add you to the guest list. The kids will be happy."

Olivia wasn't sure about Kayla. She had hoped they'd connected after she told Kayla about losing her father, but she still sensed the child didn't fully trust her. Olivia couldn't blame her. She understood how Kayla felt. "I'm sure you and Gammy have everything under control, but I'd love to help."

Jake smiled. "With ten kids currently on the guest list, we could use an extra set of hands."

As an adult, Olivia had never been to a child's birthday party. When her desire to have children started growing, she used to imagine throwing big birthday celebrations with pony rides, face painting and inflatable bouncy houses. "I'd be happy to help. Do you have anything special planned outside of the typical birthday festivities?"

"I do. I plan to take the children to the county fair. It just so happens that opening day is on their birthday."

"That sounds like perfect timing."

"I thought Kyle would burst with excitement when I told him. He's been marking the days off on our calendar hanging in the kitchen."

Olivia laughed. "What can I do to help get ready for the party?"

"Are you sure you'll have the time? Your plate seems pretty full with Myrna and Callie."

"I like to stay busy. Besides, I need to repay you for all that you've done for Gammy. Remember, I told you I'd like to help with the repairs you're doing around her house." Olivia paused and pointed to the floor. "Like this. If I had known you were coming over, I would have made a point of getting up in time to help you."

Jake slid the tape measure into the back pocket of his jeans. "No worries. You're up now. Are you ready for some coffee?"

"I work in the ER. I'm always ready for coffee." Olivia smiled.

"That's right." He palmed his forehead. "You probably live on the stuff."

"In moderation. I've seen the effects too much caffeine can have on the body."

"But a cup or two is good, right?"

Olivia nodded. "Absolutely."

"I made a fresh pot about ten minutes ago. Get yourself caffeinated and then we can go over my plans for the steps."

"Sounds like a plan." Olivia turned to head to the kitchen.

"You can let Callie out back. The kids are out there with Tank." Jake picked up his coffee from the foyer table and took a sip.

"Great. I'll be right back." Olivia continued down the hall.

The aroma of bacon lingered in the kitchen. Her stomach rumbled. Of course, Gammy had cooked breakfast for Jake and his kids. If only she'd woken up earlier, she might have enjoyed a hot meal. For now, coffee would have to do.

Radiant sunshine filled the room. It was a glorious day to be outdoors, but she'd already committed to helping Jake.

Outside, the children's laughter reminded Olivia of recess on the first warm day following a long, cold winter spent indoors. She moved to the open kitchen window. Callie followed and whimpered, longing to join in the fun. "I know, girl. I feel the same."

Olivia peered through the screen. Her heart

squeezed. A backyard filled with children was her dream. Had she missed the warning signs during their marriage that her ex-husband had changed his mind about having children? Were those years with Mark wasted? Olivia shook off the thought and reminded herself of what Gammy believed. *Choices don't determine your future. God does.* Olivia released a steadying breath. Mark was only part of her story. She couldn't allow him to put an end to her dream.

Unable to pull herself away from the window, Olivia laughed as Kayla yanked Kyle's baseball cap from his head and raced through the yard, determined to win the game of keep-away. Kyle chased his sister while Tank barked and nipped at the boy's tennis shoes.

Callie barked and scratched at the door.

"Okay, just a minute."

Olivia opened the cupboard next to the window and grabbed a large mug. She filled the cup three-quarters full and contemplated letting Callie outside without going out to greet the children herself. The last thing she wanted to do was spoil Kayla's fun.

Callie continued to scratch at the door. Olivia's stomach fluttered. She placed her sweaty palm on the door handle, but quickly dropped it to her side. She wiped her hand down her leg, knowing the fear behind her hesitation. Olivia saw herself in Kayla—a little girl who had put up walls to protect her broken heart.

Kayla's giggles filled the kitchen. Olivia opened the door to let Callie outside to join the fun. She closed it slowly. It was probably best to keep her distance. The last thing she wanted to do was steal Kayla's joy.

A slow and steady breath parted her lips. Olivia couldn't deny the truth. She was thirty-six and alone. With each passing year, her desire to have a child grew stronger. Olivia brushed away a tear racing down her cheek and turned away from a glimpse at a future that she feared would never be.

Jake pulled up the piece of carpet runner covering the last step of the staircase. Maybe the busy pattern was in style years ago, but with Myrna's eyes deteriorating, it was an accident waiting to happen. The solid carpeting he planned to place down the hardwood steps along with a colorful strip of tape on the edge of each step would provide additional contrast to ensure Myrna's safety.

The sound of dishes clattering in the kitchen surprised Jake. He assumed Olivia would have taken Callie outside to join the children and Tank. Of course, Kayla still wasn't exactly rolling out the welcome mat for Olivia.

"The coffee tastes fantastic."

Jake lifted his head from the task at hand. His pulse quickened at the sight of Olivia standing in the foyer. The sunlight streaming through the large window over the front door highlighted her delicate bone structure.

"I'm glad you like it. I brought it over this morning. It's one of my favorite blends. Myrna enjoys it, too. Are you ready to get to work?"

Olivia approached and tucked a strand of hair behind her ear. "I'm all yours. You're doing so much for Gammy. It's not fair for you to do it all alone."

"I can't think of anything I'd rather do more after all Myrna does for me and the twins."

Jake tossed the piece of rug into the pile.

"I appreciate everything you've done for Gammy. You're a good man, Jake."

He stood and dusted his hands off on his jeans. "There's nothing I wouldn't do for your grandmother. She means the world to me, like she does to you, too."

"I'm pretty sure Gammy feels the same about you."

The back screen door closed with a bang. Feet padded against the hardwood.

"Hi, Dr. Olivia!" the twins called out.

"Hello." Olivia tossed up a hand.

"Daddy, we're hungry," Kayla announced.

Jake turned with a smile. "After the big breakfast Miss Myrna cooked for you? Your tummies must be bottomless pits. Between the two of you, I think you polished off at least a dozen silver-dollar pancakes."

"That was hours ago." Kayla rolled her eyes.

"Yeah, besides, those pancakes are little. Can we go to Charlie's?" Kyle tugged on Jake's tool belt.

Jake glanced at his watch. "Well, I had planned to go into town to pick up some new light bulbs for Miss Myrna."

"Yay!" The children cheered.

Kyle stepped closer to Olivia. "Do you want to come with us?"

"Who's Charlie?" Olivia looked down at Kyle. "Is he a friend of yours?"

Kyle giggled. "No. It's a place to eat."

"Charlie's Chuck Wagon is a local diner in town. It's owned by Mary Simpson. Charlie was Mary's great-great-grandfather," Jake explained.

"They have the best cheeseburgers in the world!" Kyle looked at his father. "Not as good as yours, Daddy."

Jake ruffled the top of Kyle's head. "Thanks, son, but my burgers can't compete." He turned to Olivia. "You're welcome to come along. We can show you around town a little. If you're going to stay for a while, it might be a good idea to familiarize yourself with some of the local establishments."

Olivia chewed her lower lip. "Actually, I wanted to check out some of the local markets and also the bank."

Jake laughed. "It won't take long to check out the markets since we only have one here in Bluebell."

"I guess people shop at the big-box store instead?"

Jake had never been to Miami, but he'd read enough about it to know that it was a different world from Bluebell. It would take time for Olivia to become acclimated in a small town. "Most make do with what we have here locally. For the bigger stores, you need to travel to Denver."

"Well, since I won't be here permanently, I'm sure I'll be fine."

Jake hoped when Olivia returned home, she'd leave Myrna and Callie here in Bluebell, where they belonged. "Okay, let's feed the dogs and secure them before we hit the road."

Thirty minutes later, the foursome sat inside Charlie's Chuck Wagon. Dark wood paneling surrounded their corner booth. Peanut shells covered the hardwood flooring.

Olivia peeked over her menu. "I feel like I've stepped onto the set of a Western movie. I'm surprised there isn't one of those mechanical bulls."

"Oh, they got rid of that in the early '90s after Seth Davis nearly broke his neck. He had one too many root beers minus the root and tried to ride the bull standing up." Jake laughed.

"Cool!" Kyle exclaimed. "Maybe I can try that on the merry-go-round at the park?"

Jake tossed his son a look and shook his head. "You'll ride sitting down, young man."

"Hi, Jake. It's nice to see you and the kids."

Evelyn Simpson, Mary Simpson's older sister, had worked at Charlie's for as long as Jake could remember. She greeted the customers with a warm smile, along with a side order of the latest gossip. If you wanted to know what was going on around town, you asked Evelyn.

"Well now, who is this pretty young thing?" She cast her eyes on Olivia. "Wait a minute. You must be Myrna's granddaughter."

"She's a doctor!" Kyle announced.

Evelyn nodded. "ER, from what I hear. That's quite impressive. Bluebell isn't as exciting as Miami, but I hope you enjoy your stay. Of course, I have a sneaking suspicion you'll fall in love with our town and never want to leave."

"It's nice to meet you. I'm Olivia Hart." She extended her hand to Evelyn. "I don't have plans to stay since my home is in Florida, but I'm enjoying my visit."

"You might have a change of heart." Evelyn winked. "Now, what can I get everyone?"

"Cheeseburgers?" Jake scanned the table.

"Don't forget the fries and chocolate shakes, Daddy." Kyle bounced up and down. "You'll love the fries, Dr. Olivia. They're curly!"

"Did you get that, Evelyn?" Jake winked at the server.

Evelyn scribbled on the pad and slid the pencil behind her ear. "I'll get your orders back to Henry, pronto." She pocketed the pad and scurried toward the kitchen.

"Daddy, can I have a quarter for the jukebox?" Kyle reached his hand across the walnut tabletop.

Jake reached into the pocket of his jeans and fished out a handful of change. He eyed Kayla. She hadn't spoken a word since they'd left the house. "Kayla, do you want to play your favorite song for Miss Olivia?"

The child shrugged her shoulders.

"Come on, Kay. You always love to hear that song about Jeremiah the bullfrog." Kyle tugged on his sister's arm and took off.

Without saying a word, Kayla jumped off the seat and ran across the restaurant, chasing her brother.

Olivia kept her eyes on the children. "Kyle is protective of his sister. That's so sweet."

Jake was thankful Kyle kept a watchful eye on Kayla. "After their mother died, he thought it was his responsibility to look after her. Sometimes I think he does a better job with her than I do."

"You shouldn't be so hard on yourself. You're doing an amazing job. It can't be easy. Kayla told me you built her the clubhouse after you lost your wife."

After Laura passed away, life went on for his brothers and they went back to living their normal lives. Jake no longer knew what normal was. How could he go on without his wife? She gave him the two greatest blessings he'd ever received—his children. Laura brought joy and inspiration to his life every day. "Kayla wouldn't talk for weeks. I took her to the doctor, but he said to give her time. The more time that passed, the more helpless I became, so I built the clubhouse. When I couldn't sleep at night, I'd work on it. Constructing that little house kept my hands busy and my mind occupied. Your grandmother was staying with us and she kept the coffee coming. On those really dark days, she'd share stories about Laura. She stressed how important it was to talk about her, just like you taught Kayla, but that was so hard for me. I thought if I didn't bring her up, my pain would go away."

"And did it?"

"No, it stayed fresh. I caused a lot more pain for Kayla." Jake glanced over at the kids dancing near the jukebox. His heart warmed. "Thank you for opening my eyes to what I was doing wrong."

Olivia leaned back in the booth. "So, last night's story time must have ended well?"

Jake couldn't have asked for a more perfect night. With the children fresh out of a bubble bath, they'd cuddled up in their pajamas. The three snuggled into Jake's bed while he reminisced about their mother. "I slept better than I had in the last two years. I told the kids about the night I proposed to their mother." Jake remembered the evening as though it were yesterday.

"I'm sure they enjoyed hearing that story." Olivia's chin tilted and she tucked a stray piece of hair behind her ear. "I'd love to hear it, too."

"Really?"

Olivia nodded. "I would."

Jake smiled. "I picked up Laura at her house. I still remember the feeling I had in the pit of my stomach as I drove to her house."

"Butterflies?"

Jake shook his head. "More like bats. Not just one or two, but a swarm. I had spoken with her father the day before, so he and Laura's mother had given us their blessing, but I wasn't sure if Laura would say yes."

"How long had you been dating?"

It was difficult to remember his life without Laura. "Since the seventh grade. That's when her family moved to Virginia, where I'm from. Two weeks before the first dance of that year, a friend told me Billy Parker was going to ask Laura to be his date. I couldn't let that happen, so that day in the cafeteria, I asked her if she wanted to be my girlfriend. Of course, at that age, neither one of us really knew what that meant."

Olivia laughed. "I remember."

"We were together until we graduated from high school. That's when I realized I wanted to marry her."

"That's sweet. You married your high school sweetheart."

Jake explained to Olivia that he had sat at his desk in his bedroom the night before, mapping out his plan to propose. He even checked the time the sun would set the next day. "I had everything planned out. First, we'd go to an afternoon movie. After, a sunset picnic at Sawyer's Canyon. That's where I wanted to propose to her. At the movie theater, I remember her asking me what was wrong. I was so nervous I spilled our jumbo bucket of popcorn. When she passed me the box of sour balls, I dropped it, and the candies flew all over the floor."

Olivia covered her mouth before a giggle escaped.

"Yeah, there I was, the star quarterback, and I was so nervous I couldn't even hold on to a little box of candy." Jake paused and looked up at Olivia. Her smile lit up her entire face. "Trust me, it gets worse."

"I have a feeling it has a happy ending, though." Olivia picked at the folded napkin on the table.

"After the movie, we went outside. The film had run a little longer than the guide had stated. I still needed to make the twenty-minute drive to the canyon, but the sun was setting fast."

Olivia moved toward the edge of her seat. "You made it, didn't you?"

"Well, I had to hurry. I opened the door for Laura and then I raced around to the other side of the car. I stumbled on a rock in the street and dropped the car keys." Jake paused, picked up his glass of water and took a sip.

"And?"

"The keys bounced down inside of the sewer."

Olivia's brown eyes doubled in size. "Oh, no!"

"It gets worse." Jake shook his head. "Within seconds, the rain came. That was something my teenage brain didn't consider when making my plan. I forgot to check the weather."

Olivia stifled a laugh.

"Laura unlocked the driver's-side door so at least I could get inside. For the next half hour, it poured. Water gushed down the street and into the sewer."

"And the keys?" Olivia's brow arched.

"Never found them."

"But you still proposed, right?"

"Well, that's where the story takes another twist. Our geometry teacher, Mr. Preston, pulled up. After I told him what happened, he drove me and Laura home."

"I'm sorry your plan didn't work out that night. Did you surprise her another time?"

"Actually, her mother did." Jake laughed.

"What happened?"

"By the time we arrived at her parents' house, the rain had stopped. When we pulled into the driveway, Laura's mother came running from the house. You would have thought there was a fire. We got out of the car and her mother grabbed Laura in her arms and cried. She told her how happy she was that we were going to get married."

"No! Oh, Jake!" Olivia couldn't hold back her laughter. "I'm so sorry."

Jake burst out laughing. "It was like being in a sitcom. Her mother was grabbing her hand and looking for the ring. Of course, at first, Laura was clueless. Then her father came out and welcomed me into the family. In the end, we all had a good laugh about it. Her parents were ecstatic because they got to see the proposal live."

"So you asked her that night?"

"Yep, right there in the driveway."

Olivia sat back. "That's the best proposal story I've ever heard."

For a moment, Jake remained silent. In less than twenty-four hours, for the second time, talking about Laura had come easy for him.

Olivia reached across the table and rested her hand on top of Jake's. "Are you okay?"

He released a long breath and looked at their hands. "Life doesn't always go as we plan, does it?"

Olivia shook her head. "I know mine hasn't."

Jake watched the smile Olivia had worn while he'd shared the proposal story slip away.

"Thank you for listening."

"I appreciate you sharing the story with me."

Silence hung in the air as the server approached with their orders.

"Okay, I've got two burgers with double cheese."

Olivia flinched and quickly pulled away her hand.

For a split second, Jake longed to feel her touch again, but out of respect for Laura, he forced the thought away.

Chapter Eight

"I've made a list of the things we need to pick up for Kayla and Kyle's birthday party." Myrna flipped through the pages of a brown leather journal.

Olivia approached the light signal and eased her foot off the accelerator. "I wish I had one-half of your organizational skills, Gammy."

"I just write everything down in here." She lifted the journal. "I have boxes of these at home filled with every store list, appointment, Bible study, recipe and thoughts from the day. You name it and it's recorded."

Olivia worried what Gammy would do when she could no longer see to write about her daily events. It was obviously an important ritual. Maybe she could use the recording feature on her cell phone. "So, what's first on the list?"

"Hank Garrison will drop off the tents tomorrow afternoon. There's only a slight chance of rain in the forecast for Saturday, but Jake thought it was best to play it safe. Hank and his crew will set up the tents in front of the house."

"I thought the party was going to be at the fairgrounds?" One year, Olivia and her father attended the Colorado State Fair and made some of her fondest memories. Her mother had planned to attend, but she'd come down with the flu. Olivia remembered her father had let her eat as much cotton candy as her stomach could hold. "I remember seeing the dog stunt show. It was hilarious. Daddy and I laughed so hard our stomachs hurt."

Gammy smiled. "It makes me happy when you recall the good times."

Olivia only wished she'd had more time to create memories with him.

"Make a left here, dear." Myrna pointed to Garrison's Mercantile Company.

Olivia hit the turn signal.

"I guess Jake didn't mention that the twins' party is an all-day event. Garrison's will have most of what we need." She closed her journal and slipped it inside her purse. "We celebrate big here in Bluebell. Once you get a taste of it, you won't want to leave." Myrna laughed. "We'll spend the morning and afternoon at the fair. After, we'll come back to Jake's place for a cookout, fireworks and other activities."

"Sounds like fun, but a lot of work for Jake."

Myrna swatted her hand. "He'd do anything for those kids. Besides, practically the entire town has volunteered to help. In fact, I put you in charge of baking the cakes. We'll pick up the ingredients today."

Olivia loved to bake, but once she went to work in the ER, she began purchasing her baked goods. She navigated the SUV into an open parking spot in front of the store. "Of course I will. What's their favorite?"

"They both love my recipe for German chocolate cake. It's been in the family for generations."

Olivia smiled. "I remember. You baked it when you and Pops came to stay with me and Mom."

"It was your father's favorite." Myrna unfastened her seat belt and patted Olivia's hand. "Let's only think good thoughts today."

"That sounds like a plan."

Olivia stepped inside the store and took in the rustic surroundings. The uneven floorboards and rough wood walls gave the mercantile a warm and welcoming feel. It was the complete opposite of the high-end boutiques with modern designs that lined the streets of Miami.

The aroma of cedar sent a flood of memories through her. She pictured the chest that sat at the foot of her childhood bed. After her father died, she'd packed away pictures and special gifts he'd given her. Over the years, the chest had traveled with Olivia as she moved from one home to another.

"Look who's here."

Olivia spotted a petite, gray-haired woman coming from the back room and walking around the checkout counter at a swift pace. An oversize box in her arms didn't hinder her speed. Every strand of her short silver hair was in place, as though she'd just returned from the hairdresser.

"This is Nellie Garrison, Hank's wife and co-owner of the mercantile." Gammy made the introduction. "Nellie, this is my granddaughter, Olivia."

The woman set the box on the counter and approached her customers. "I'd recognize that beautiful face anywhere." Nellie placed her hands on Olivia's cheeks. "Your grandmother is so proud of you. She's shared many photographs of you. I knew who you were the moment you walked in. I'm glad you finally got away from that ER and made it to Bluebell. You'll never want to leave."

What was it about this place? It was like everyone who lived in town worked for the chamber of commerce. Was there something about Bluebell Olivia couldn't see? "My work is back in Miami, so I'll only be here long enough to convince Gammy it's time for someone to take care of her."

"Is she still on that silly idea?" Nellie tugged on Myrna's arm and laughed. "There's no one in this town who would think twice about helping your grandmother, so there's no need to worry about her. Of course, if you moved to Bluebell, you could keep a close eye on her yourself," Nellie said with a wink.

Olivia bit her tongue to keep the peace. Her stomach twisted as she realized it wasn't only Gammy she'd have to convince that moving would be in her best interest. The entire community might be an obstacle for her. But if she didn't feel confident in Callie's abilities, Olivia would have no option but to carry out her original plan.

The front door swooshed behind them.

"Look who's here." Nellie nodded her head toward the customer.

Olivia spun on her heel in time to see Jake strolling into the store. His boots scraped across the hardwood. His normally straight posture was gone and instead he appeared hunched. Underneath his dark brown cowboy hat, Olivia saw lines crinkling along his forehead.

"Jake, is everything okay?" Myrna asked.

She hadn't imagined it. Even Gammy noticed the weight Jake carried.

"Jake," Olivia asked, "is everything okay?"

"I don't want to interrupt…"

Nellie took advantage of his brief pause. "I'm just getting to know Myrna's gorgeous granddaughter. You should show her around Bluebell!"

Olivia's face warmed. She quickly changed the subject to the twins' birthday. "Gammy and I just stopped in to pick up some things for the party."

Jake's expression darkened further. "That's what I wanted to talk with Myrna about."

Nellie took Olivia's hand. "We'll leave you two alone to talk."

"No, I'd like to get all of your opinions." Jake removed his hat and raked his hand through his hair.

"What is it, Jake? I'm worried," Myrna said.

"Kayla came home from school today and announced she wasn't going to her birthday party." Jake slipped his hands into the back pockets of his mud-splattered jeans.

"Oh, my stars, that's the silliest thing I've ever heard." Nellie pulled out a stool. "Here, dear, take a seat." She patted her hand against the larch wood stool next to the counter. "It sounds like you need a good cup of strong coffee." Nellie scurried to the back room, but Jake didn't sit. Instead, he paced the floor.

Myrna cleared her throat. "Does Kyle have any idea why his sister had this sudden change of heart? Just last week, Kayla was so excited about the party. She'd chattered endlessly about all the different animals she wanted to see at the fair."

Jake shook his head. "Kyle said during recess he saw a couple of Kayla's friends whispering and pointing at her while she was getting a drink from the water fountain. A couple of minutes later, Kayla ran to the far side of the playground and hid behind a tree. He went to check on her, but she wouldn't talk to him."

"Poor Kayla. Sometimes children can be cruel when they decide to gang up on one of their friends," Myrna said.

Olivia saw the pain in Jake's eyes.

"I suspect the teasing may have been about the mother-daughter fashion show. Kyle mentioned it recently, but I kind of brushed it off because I didn't hear more about it." Jake sighed.

Nellie crossed the room with a tray of cups, along with a carafe of coffee. "I got an email the other day from my women's club about volunteering for the fashion show. I signed up. It sounded like fun."

Jake dipped his chin. "Maybe not for a little girl who lost her mother. I'm afraid this event is triggering a lot of sad memories for Kayla."

Olivia's heart ached for Kayla. A few months after her father passed away, her elementary school hosted a father-daughter dance for all grades. Weeks before the event, her girlfriends talked nonstop about what they'd wear and how their dads were all taking them out to a fancy, grown-up dinner.

"You okay?" Gammy whispered to Olivia.

Olivia nodded and smiled. She found comfort in knowing that her grandmother remembered the dance as well. If it hadn't been for Gammy, that evening would have been the worst night of her life. Instead of the dance, they got dressed up and went to the movies. After, Gammy took her to the most expensive restaurant in town. It was the first time Olivia had eaten at a table draped with a linen tablecloth and with a candle as the centerpiece. For one night, thanks to her grandmother, the pain of losing her father waned.

"The kids raced out of the house so fast when the bus honked its horn for school this morning, I wasn't able to talk with Kayla. But after they left, I went up to their rooms to strip the sheets from their beds and I found this under Kayla's mattress. It's the flyer announcing the fashion show." Jake slipped a folded piece of paper from his back pocket and passed it to Myrna.

Olivia watched as Gammy opened the paper and nodded. "There's no doubt about it. It's the fashion show that has Kayla upset. We'll have to put our heads together to come up with an idea to help her."

"I can take her." The words spilled out of Olivia's mouth before her brain could process the offer. She was usually an overthinker, always weighing the pros and cons of her ideas before speaking or acting.

"That's a wonderful idea." Gammy wasted no time with her response. She rested her hand on Olivia's arm.

The touch brought her back into the moment. Was this the right thing to do? What made her think Kayla would even want to go with her? Although they had a moment of connection in Kayla's clubhouse, their relationship appeared to have regressed to its original state when they first met. It was obvious Kayla felt threatened by her presence. In her mind, Olivia was trying to replace her mother.

"I appreciate the offer, but I'm not sure if that's a good idea." Jake kept a close eye on Olivia.

Now was her opportunity to back out. But as

much as Olivia wanted to run out of the store and take the offer with her, her heart had a different idea. Olivia had been in Kayla's situation. She knew the agony of losing a parent. How could she walk away?

"You've come a long way." Olivia scratched Callie underneath her collar and, with the other hand, fed her a treat.

After skipping lunch with Gammy on Friday, Olivia packed up Callie and headed to Jake's place. She wanted to work with the pup before camp started.

"Not quite."

Olivia looked up and squinted into the late-afternoon sun. Jake towered over her, twisting a piece of straw between his teeth. She wasn't sure if there were any magazines that featured cowboys, but if so, Jake could be on the cover.

"Why would you say that?"

Jake squatted and rubbed Callie's head. "I think we've got our hands full with this little one."

"Are you saying Callie can't help Gammy? I remember you said some dogs don't have what it takes to work as service animals."

"That's true, but I still have hope." He picked up Callie and rubbed his nose into her coat. "It's okay, girl. I believe in you."

Callie covered Jake's face with sloppy kisses. "You certainly have a way with her." Olivia laughed.

"I wish I could say the same about Kayla."

Olivia hoped Kayla would change her mind about attending her birthday party, but according to Gammy, she hadn't mentioned it.

"It's obvious you mean the world to her. Losing a parent is a lot for a child to handle, but it's a blessing Kayla and Kyle have each other. After my dad died, I'd pretend my stuffed animals were my siblings, so I could have someone to talk to." Olivia stood.

Jake reached out and placed his hand on Olivia's arm. "Thanks for sharing that with me. I appreciate it."

A warm sensation traveled up her arm. She moved her eyes toward his hand. "You're welcome."

"Daddy! We're home!" Kyle called out from across the pasture.

Jake's hand pulled away and Olivia looked up. His eyes remained fixated on her as though neither wanted to be the first to look away. Warmth spread across her face. What exactly was happening? She'd missed lunch. Maybe it was her blood sugar dropping. That had to be the reason.

"I aced my spelling test!" Kyle smiled, revealing a missing front tooth.

"That's wonderful, son. Congratulations."

"Hey, when did that happen?" Olivia pointed at Kyle's mouth. She looked over and noticed Kayla walking slowly toward them with her head down.

"This morning! Isn't it cool? Daddy said if I put it under my pillow tonight, I might get a surprise."

Kayla joined them but remained silent.

"Did you have a good day, sweetie?" Jake asked.

Kayla shrugged her shoulders.

Olivia noticed the redness around her eyes.

"Run inside and change. I need your help to set up the cones for camp."

"I'll be right back," Kyle called out over his shoulder as he sped toward the house.

"Daddy, do I have to help with camp today?"

"What's wrong? You're not sick, are you?" Jake brushed Kayla's hair away and placed his hand on her forehead. "Cool as a cucumber."

"I feel okay."

Jake's brow arched. "Did you do poorly on your spelling test?"

Kayla shook her head. "I didn't miss any words."

"That's great, sweetie. Then why so glum?"

Kayla glanced at Olivia before turning her attention back to the ground.

Olivia could see Kayla was upset, but her gut

told her it had nothing to do with a spelling test. It was more. When Kayla's eyes met hers for a second time, Olivia sensed maybe Kayla wanted to talk, but not necessarily to her father.

"Sweetie?" Jake kept a close eye on his daughter. "Do you want to talk about what's bothering you?"

Olivia took a step back. "I'm going to take Callie and get her some water. You two talk."

"No!" Kayla snapped. Her face turned red.

Jake turned to Olivia, then back to Kayla. "I can't help you if you don't talk to me."

Kayla kicked her tennis shoe into the ground and bit her lip. "It's just— Forget it. You wouldn't understand." Kayla pivoted and ran across the yard to her clubhouse.

Jake slid his hands into his back pockets. "What am I missing here?"

"You're just being a guy."

Jake sighed. "That's the only thing I know how to be." He scratched his head and looked toward the clubhouse.

"Sometimes a girl needs—"

"Her mother. Is that what you think this is about? Girl talk?"

A look of understanding washed over Jake's face. He was a good father and sensitive to his daughter's needs. "Exactly. May I?" She pointed at the clubhouse.

"Would you?"

"Of course I will." Olivia handed Callie's leash to Jake.

Jake took the leather strap. "Thank you."

"Don't thank me yet." Olivia smiled and headed across the yard.

The closer she got to the little pink house, the more her stomach knotted. Olivia's steps slowed. What if it had all been a mistake and Kayla didn't want to talk with her? It was a chance she would have to take. Olivia had seen the pain in Kayla's eyes. She couldn't allow her to keep everything bottled up. It wasn't healthy.

Outside the door of the clubhouse, Olivia leaned close to the little building, but no sound came from the other side. She gently tapped her knuckles against the door. "Kayla. May I come in?"

Olivia waited in silence. She fought the urge to push the door open, take Kayla into her arms and tell her everything would be okay. She had to remain patient. The last thing Olivia wanted to do was push Kayla even further away.

The second she raised her hand to knock again, the door slowly opened.

"I was hoping you'd come." Kayla peered around the door.

Olivia's breath hitched. Kayla wanted her there? The child's eyes looked redder than earlier. Clutched in her left hand was the photograph of her mother.

Olivia's heart broke as memories of her father and how she'd felt after he died flooded her mind. "Do you want some company?"

Kayla pulled the door open wider. Olivia stepped inside.

A music box played. Kayla moved toward the table with two chairs. Olivia followed behind, recognizing the song. "Bridge Over Troubled Water."

Frozen, Olivia stared at the music box in the middle of the table. She closed her eyes and saw her mother and father dancing in the kitchen. It was the only time Olivia had ever seen her parents holding each other. Olivia could still picture the joyful smiles on their faces. Her mother had giggled softly when her father whispered something in her ear. After her father died, Olivia never heard her mother giggle again.

"Dr. Olivia, are you okay?"

Kayla's voice startled her back into the moment. "Yes. I'm sorry."

"It's okay." Kayla looked at the music box. "Do you know that song?"

Olivia nodded. "Yes. I remember my parents dancing to it."

Kayla turned her attention to the picture frame. "It was my mommy's favorite song. She gave me this music box the day after she told me I was going to have another brother."

"That's a very special gift."

Kayla put the picture frame on the table and picked up the music box. "She shouldn't have given it to me."

"Why would you say that? I'm sure your mommy bought it special just for you."

She ran her tiny fingers around the gold-plated casing. "I was mean to her."

"Why, sweetie?"

Kayla bit her lower lip. "I didn't want another brother, or another sibling." She tipped her head down. "Kyle was born first. If Mommy had another kid, I wouldn't be her baby anymore."

"And you were afraid she might not love you as much anymore?"

Kayla nodded. "But I did something bad."

Olivia couldn't imagine Kayla doing anything bad outside of the ordinary things that children did. "Maybe it's not as bad as you think." Olivia pulled out a chair for Kayla and then took the other seat. Outside the clubhouse, dogs barked. Olivia glanced at her watch. They had twenty minutes before camp began. "Do you want to tell me what happened?" She reached across the table and took Kayla's hand.

"I prayed." Kayla spoke barely above a whisper.

"Well, that doesn't sound too bad."

"I asked God to make me Mommy's baby forever."

Olivia's stomach twisted. Kayla blamed herself for the death of her mother and baby brother.

"It was my fault they died."

"Sweetie, you can't blame yourself for that. Your mommy had a medical emergency. What happened to her and your brother had nothing to do with your prayers."

Kayla's brow crinkled. "Really?"

"I promise." She gave Kayla's hand a squeeze.

"Last week, I told Cindy, my best friend, about my prayer, and she told Missy, the mean girl in my class. Yesterday, on the playground, Missy told me it was my fault."

That was why Kayla didn't want to go to her party. It wasn't only because of the fashion show.

"I never told my daddy. I thought he'd get mad at me."

Olivia offered a small smile and leaned in. "You can always tell your daddy anything. He might get upset or disappointed, but he'll never stop loving you."

Kayla wiped at the tear racing down her cheek. She looked up. "Kind of like God?" Her eyebrows drew together. "I learned in Bible school that God will love me no matter how much I mess up. Is that true?"

Olivia nodded. "Yes, thankfully it is the truth. And your daddy will always love you too, no matter what you do."

A tiny smile parted Kayla's mouth. She sprang from the chair and wrapped her arms tight around Olivia's waist. "Thank you for making me feel better. I think I'll tell my daddy about my mean prayer tonight when we say our prayers together."

Olivia embraced Kayla and closed her eyes, savoring the connection. "I think that would be the perfect time."

Kayla pulled back. "You know what else I'm going to tell him?"

"What's that?" Olivia gently brushed a strand of hair away from Kayla's face.

"I'm going to tell Daddy that I'm going to my party tomorrow." She grinned.

"That will make him very happy." Olivia checked her watch. "Maybe you should go help your daddy get ready for camp?"

"Okay." Kayla gave Olivia another quick hug.

"I'll be there in a minute," Olivia added.

Kayla skipped out the door, taking a piece of Olivia's heart with her. Olivia wrapped her arms around her body. If only she could forget the past so easily. A painful lump formed in her throat. She picked up the music box, turned it over and wound the key. Thoughts flooded her mind as the familiar song played. She recalled her father's death, her failed marriage, and thought about a possible future without children. Alone in the clubhouse, she rested her head on the table and wept.

"Wow! This is so cool!" Kyle squeezed Jake's right hand and bounced on his toes.

Jake couldn't have asked for better weather. The prediction of rain earlier in the week had failed to materialize. The tents Hank Garrison set up at the house weren't necessary unless people wanted to escape the bright sunshine.

"Where are we going to meet everyone, Daddy?" Kayla held tight on to Jake's left hand.

Jake still didn't know what Olivia had said yesterday in the clubhouse, but he was thankful she had somehow convinced Kayla to attend her seventh birthday party.

"We have some tables set up near the concession area." He and Myrna had concluded being close to the food would be the best place for the party guests to gather. The kids and their parents could come and go while having a home base to rest or grab something to eat.

"That's good because I'm hungry," said Kyle.

"You're always hungry." Kayla rolled her eyes at her brother.

Jake smiled at his children's banter. Although

today was a day to celebrate, he couldn't help but think about Laura and the baby. Early this morning, before the kids were out of bed, Jake had gone for a long walk on his property. He thanked God for all his blessings and prayed for the strength to remain present for this special day for his children. Over breakfast, the children shared memories of their mother.

"Look over there at the big sign, Kayla. That's for us!"

"Wow! Cool!" Kayla ran toward the sign. Kyle pulled his hand free from Jake's grip and followed his sister.

Jake had ordered a personalized "Happy Birthday" banner designed by a Denver company he'd found on the internet. It showcased his children's names in large block-style lettering. It thrilled Jake to see the children so happy.

A group of people swarmed below the banner. Judging by the size of the crowd, it looked like everyone had already arrived. His shoulders slouched when he didn't see any sign of Olivia.

"Daddy!" Kyle raced to his father's side. "Uncle Logan said he and Uncle Cody want to take us to the rodeo. Can we go?"

"Of course you can, but what about the stunt dogs? That's going to start at the same time." Jake had carefully studied the schedule of events.

He wanted to make sure Kyle and Kayla didn't miss a thing.

"I'd rather see the bull riders. I see dogs all the time." He giggled.

Jake recalled growing up in Whispering Slopes in the Shenandoah Valley of Virginia. His parents took him and his brothers to the state fair, where seeing everything was impossible. Kyle was smart to choose something new. "Today is your day, so you get to decide, but first it's important for us to greet your guests. They're here to celebrate with you and your sister."

Kyle pulled his father toward the group. The aroma of sugary funnel cake teased his sweet tooth. Jake spotted Olivia. He narrowed his eyes and watched her talking with his younger brother Logan. He was taken aback by how beautiful she looked with her hair pulled back in a ponytail and a cowboy hat on her head. It appeared the city doctor was fitting right in with the locals.

Logan noticed Jake's arrival first. "Hey, bud, I thought you were going to miss your own kids' party," Logan joked.

Jake smiled. "Welcome back. How was the trip?"

"Alaska was amazing. Cody is already talking about going back. Our flight was late getting in last night, so we're both a little worn out."

"I'm sure you are. I appreciate you both coming to celebrate today," Jake said.

"We wouldn't have missed it." Logan palmed Jake's shoulder. "I was just getting to know Myrna's granddaughter. We could use a doctor like her in town. I've heard some chatter that Dr. Dickerson might be retiring."

Jake shook his head. "Those beauty shop women gossip too much. Doc Dickerson will keep practicing medicine as long as he's upright."

"You're probably right." Logan tipped his hat to Olivia. "It was a pleasure talking to you. I better start rounding up the kids who want to go to the rodeo. Are you interested in going?"

Olivia glanced in Jake's direction. "Is everyone going as a group?"

"No. While we're here, everyone is kind of doing their own thing. There's too much to see to please everyone. Later at the ranch, we'll have more organized events." Jake placed his hand on his brother's shoulder. "I had a little surprise planned for Olivia, which is scheduled to begin in fifteen minutes. So, if she's game, we'll pass. Thanks for taking the twins, buddy."

"Sounds good. A couple of parents are going along, so don't worry about me losing any of the kids." Logan laughed, turned on his heel and moved to the group of parents congregated around one of the picnic tables.

Olivia cleared her throat. "You probably don't know this, but I'm not big on surprises. I'm more of a routine person."

"I never would have guessed." Jake nudged her arm. "Sometimes it's good to be spontaneous and not follow a schedule."

Olivia placed her hands on her hips. "You sound like Gammy. Just the other day, she said that exact thing to me."

"Well, you are on vacation, aren't you? Maybe now is a good time to start some new habits. Make some changes that might make you happier."

"What makes you think I'm not happy? Did Gammy say something to you?"

The last thing he wanted to do today was upset her. "I'm sorry. Maybe my advice was out of line. I know how precious life is, that's all. I have a habit of trying to make sure people I care about don't take life for granted. Putting things off until they fit into your schedule isn't the way to live. There's no guarantee for a tomorrow."

A look of understanding crossed Olivia's face. "You're right. I am on vacation, after all. What better time is there to do things a little spur of the moment?"

"There you go." Jake smiled. "By the way, nice hat." He winked.

She fingered the brim and her cheeks flushed.

"Gammy bought it for me." She looked down at her feet. "She purchased the boots, too. Do I look silly?"

That was not how Jake would describe her. Between the hat, the faded jeans and the pair of cowboy boots, she was the prettiest cowgirl he'd seen in a long time. "You look great. No one would ever know you're a city girl."

Olivia's eyes widened. Her hand cupped her cheek. "I just realized this all plays into Gammy's grand plan to keep me here in Bluebell."

Jake laughed. "I wouldn't worry. It will take more than some Western clothing for you to uproot your life and move."

"You're right. Miami is my home. That will never change."

Olivia's words ignited a sinking feeling in his stomach. While they headed toward the arena to watch the dog stunt show, Jake struggled to brush off the disappointment Olivia's comment had sparked. Today was a day to celebrate the twins' birthday. This wasn't the time to lose his heart to a woman who lived a couple thousand miles away and wanted children of her own. Having more children wasn't part of his plan.

Chapter Nine

From the moment Olivia had arrived on the grounds with Gammy, a sense of nostalgia consumed her. She loved everything about the fair. And the best part was the day had just begun. The cheerful sounds of children enjoying themselves, the food trucks lining the trampled grass, the air filled with the sweet smells of treats, all brought back wonderful memories of the trip to the fair with her father. Jake's advice from earlier entered her mind. For most of her adult life, she'd allowed work to dominate both her schedule and her ability to enjoy the gift of life. She could never imagine the pain Jake had endured. If anyone understood the reason to live each day as if it were your last, it was Jake Beckett.

"I can't believe you're not asking where I'm taking you. I thought you'd want to pull out your cell phone and put it on your schedule."

Jake playfully nudged his arm against Olivia, making her keenly aware of his broad shoulders. "Stop it." She pushed back against him, giggling like a child. "I've decided my phone is off-limits today."

"Good for you. But I know from experience, sometimes old habits are hard to break."

"I'll keep that in mind." Olivia knew all too well about breaking habits. Lately, she'd been more guarded of her time off from the hospital. At first it was difficult to say no to colleagues who once relied on her to cover when she wasn't on the schedule. But now she looked forward to those days where she was able to do something for herself. Going to a coffee shop and reading for hours was her latest obsession. "So, are you going to tell me where we're headed?"

"You're worse than the twins." Jake laughed. "Are we there yet?" His voice mimicked the twins' higher voices.

Olivia rolled her eyes and laughed. A group of senior women approached from the other direction.

"Hello, Jake."

"Hi, Mrs. Hinton. I hope you ladies are enjoying yourselves."

"Yes, we are. It looks like you are, too." The elderly woman winked as she and the others moved toward the line at the cotton candy vendor.

Since their ten-minute walk to wherever they were going began, Olivia noted that everyone who passed seemed to stop and say something to Jake. "Is there anyone you don't know?"

"That's the best part about living in a small town. I couldn't imagine raising my children anywhere but Bluebell." Jake stopped at the metal gate that surrounded an enclosed building. "We're here."

Olivia's heart raced. She didn't know what was behind the gate, but the anticipation was exhilarating. "Can you tell me now?"

Jake turned, wearing a smile. "We're going to watch the stunt dogs perform."

For a second, Olivia had to remind herself to breathe. Her mouth was dry. She struggled to find the right words.

Jake gently placed his hand on her shoulder. "Are you okay?"

Olivia bit her lower lip. Tears peppered her eyelashes.

"What is it? I thought you'd enjoy this."

Olivia shook her head. "I haven't seen the stunt dogs since I was a kid. They were my dad's favorite."

"Your grandmother mentioned it. That's why I thought you'd like to come to the show."

Jake's thoughtfulness was endearing. She'd forgotten she'd mentioned to Gammy about going to the dog show with her dad. She inhaled a deep breath. "I'd love to go with you."

"I'm happy to hear that. Shall we?" Jake gently clasped her hand, creating a reaction she couldn't quite identify. Whatever it was, she liked it.

Ten minutes later, Olivia sat alone in the stands while Jake was off getting popcorn. He said one of the best parts about seeing the show was the butter-laden popcorn. She couldn't argue with that. She even ordered a diet soda. After all, she was on vacation.

Her shoulders relaxed as she took in the crowd of mostly children with their parents. A longing tried to take hold, but she forced it aside. Today was a day to enjoy life. She refused to dwell on the past.

Olivia spotted Jake working his way through the crowd, carrying a cardboard tray with their snacks. Her pulse ticked up a few beats. Western-style clothing was never her thing, but Jake sure looked good in his long-sleeved denim shirt with silver buttons down the front, paired with khakis. As he moved toward their seats, she couldn't ignore the way the shirt brought out the blue in his eyes.

"Okay, I got buttered popcorn and your diet soda. I think we have a couple of minutes before the show starts." He settled in the seat next to her and passed the drink.

Olivia put the straw between her lips. She drank as though she'd been in the desert for days, while sneaking peeks at his freshly shaven face.

"You are hooked on that stuff. I think you'll need a refill before the show starts." He laughed.

She wasn't sure if it was the syrupy sweet taste or the carbonation of the soda, but whatever it was, the cool drink settled her nerves. Olivia didn't recall ever feeling nervous during their classes at camp. Today, something seemed different. She was relieved when the announcer came over the loudspeaker to say the show would start in a few minutes.

Jake settled the tub of popcorn on his right knee and helped himself. "The stuff is great." He crammed a handful into his mouth.

Olivia reached inside the bucket and grabbed an equally large handful. "I better eat up because it looks like it will be gone before the show even gets started," she teased.

"Don't worry. They have free refills." Jake laughed.

"You better pace yourself." Olivia smiled, feeling more at ease with her one-on-one time with Jake as their conversation continued.

"Are you kidding? When I was little, I could eat this stuff all day." He raised the tub and took another handful.

Olivia scanned the program she'd picked up on the way inside. "This looks like a great lineup of stunts. I guess dogs have gotten smarter since I was a kid. I remember the juggling. It was hilarious, but also impressive. I never understood how they trained the dogs to do that."

"What about the dancing? Last year two Border collies did the tango. I tried to get Tank to do it, but he didn't want any part of it."

Jake's comment triggered a fond memory of her father. She closed her eyes for a moment. "Once, when I was little, my dad took me to a minor-league baseball game. Like my mother, I thought baseball was boring, but if I was with my dad, I was happy to go. Before they threw out the first pitch, a group of Jack Russell stunt dogs performed. I'll never forget it. I didn't know dogs could jump so high. They were even jumping rope. When we got home after the game, I remember my dad had convinced himself he could teach our dog, Tootie, to do the same."

"And did he?"

Olivia shook her head. "Tootie was a one-hundred-plus-pound Saint Bernard. What do you think?"

Jake laughed. "Excuse me for a second. My phone is vibrating." He reached into his back pocket and pulled out the device.

Olivia watched while Jake tapped the screen to open a text message.

He jumped to his feet. "I have to go. Logan said Kayla is upset."

Olivia stood.

"No, you stay and watch the show. I know how much it means to you."

That was true. Watching the stunt dogs was a trip down memory lane for Olivia, but Kayla's well-being meant more. "If you don't mind, I'd rather go with you."

"I don't mind at all. Lately, it seems like you're able to handle Kayla's issues better than I am. Let's go."

Outside of the building, Olivia heard the announcer introducing the first stunt dog. The laughter grew distant as they moved at a brisk pace toward the rodeo venue.

Moments later, Olivia spotted Logan. He jogged in their direction. Kyle trailed behind.

"Where's Kayla?" Jake scanned the area.

"She's inside the women's bathroom." Logan pointed to a nearby toilet rental as Kyle caught up with the group.

"Is she sick?"

"No, Daddy. It was that mean ole Missy. She was teasing Kayla again about the fashion show," Kyle explained.

"Before the show started, the kids went outside to get a snow cone. Missy and some other girls were in line. Kyle came back inside to tell me Kayla had locked herself in the bathroom and that's when I texted you. I'm sorry, man. I should have gone with them to get the snack." Logan rubbed the side of his temple.

"It's not your fault. This fashion show has had Kayla upset for over a week. Maybe I need to speak with Missy's mother. I know kids tease each other, but this is a sensitive issue for Kayla."

Logan nodded his agreement.

Olivia's chest tightened. She glanced toward the bathroom. "Would you like for me to talk to her?"

"Yeah, if anyone can get her to come out, it's Dr. Olivia," Kyle added.

Jake agreed with his son. He turned to Olivia. "Like I said earlier, lately Kayla seems to respond better to you," Jake said.

Olivia rested her hand on Jake's arm. "Don't take offense. I'm sure you've tried your best. It may be easier for her to talk to another female. After my father died, the mean girls chased me into hiding many times."

Kyle moved closer to Olivia. "I'm sorry you got teased, Dr. Olivia."

Olivia's heart squeezed. "Thank you, Kyle."

She patted his shoulder. "Let me get Kayla and maybe we can all watch the rodeo together."

"That sounds like a great idea. We'll just hang out here for a while," Jake said.

"But, Daddy, I never got my snow cone. Can we get one now? We can get one for Kayla when she comes out of the bathroom." Kyle tugged on Jake's hand.

"Sure." Jake looked at Olivia. "We'll meet back here?"

"Hopefully we won't be too long." Olivia turned and headed toward the restrooms. She sent up a silent prayer to be able to comfort Kayla and convince her to come out of the restroom and enjoy the fair.

Outside the door to the restroom, Olivia raised her hand and knocked. "Kayla, can you open the door, sweetie? It's Dr. Olivia." She scanned the area surrounding the two bathrooms for signs of Missy or any other children. "There's no one here except for me. I'd like to talk to you, but I'd rather see your face than talk to a door."

A soft giggle came through the vent at the top of the bathroom. This was promising. "Your daddy told me how word spreads in a small town. Can you imagine what people would think if they heard the lady from Florida talks to toilets?"

Another giggle sounded, but this time the

door slowly opened. Kayla cautiously stepped outside. Her eyes were red and swollen. She hesitated for a moment before lunging into Olivia's arms.

The lump in Olivia's throat prevented any words from escaping her lips. Instead, she clung to the child like her life depended on it. At that moment, it did. Nothing else mattered but to protect Kayla and lessen the pain of losing her mother. Olivia had carried the same pain throughout her childhood and into her adult years. Yet the time spent with Kayla seemed to ease the heartache.

"Missy is so mean." Kayla sniffled and choked on her words. "She ruined my birthday."

"Let's go sit over there." Olivia pointed to a bench perched under an old weeping willow tree.

Kayla loosened her arms from around Olivia's waist but kept hold of her hand. They walked to the tree and took a seat.

"Do you want to tell me what happened earlier?"

Kayla inched closer to Olivia. "Missy said I wear boy clothes because I don't have a mommy to teach me."

Olivia's stomach clenched at the cruelty Kayla had experienced. "That wasn't nice of her to say that to you, sweetie. Sometimes words have more power than we realize. I'm not excusing Missy, but I don't think she's learned that lesson. We have to be careful when we choose our words. When I was a little girl, Gammy always told me sometimes it's best to say nothing." Olivia wasn't sure if Kayla understood. After Olivia's father died, a couple of kids at her school spoke horrible words to her. They said she should have done something when she'd come home from school and found her father on the floor. They told her his death was her fault.

"Like when Daddy says to hold my tongue?" Kayla nuzzled her head against Olivia's side.

Olivia smiled. "Exactly."

"Yeah, sometimes I probably say things I shouldn't, especially to Kyle." Kayla wiped her eyes and looked up. "I'm sorry, Dr. Olivia."

"For what, sweetie?"

"I said some mean things to you when you first got here."

Olivia ran her fingers through the back of Kayla's hair. "It's all forgotten." She kissed the top of her head, inhaling the sweet scent of her shampoo.

"I'm glad you came to get me. You made me feel better."

"Well, today is your special day. You shouldn't spend it hiding."

Kayla nodded. "It wasn't the best place to hide. It didn't smell too good in there."

Olivia laughed. "I'm sure it didn't. Are you ready to join the others and watch the rodeo?"

Kayla jumped off the bench. "Can I ask you something first?"

"What is it, sweetie?"

Kayla pushed the toe of her red tennis shoe into the grass. "Will you take me to the fashion show?"

"I didn't think you had any interest in watching the show."

"I don't want to watch. I want to be in it with you." Kayla twisted a strand of her hair.

Excitement coursed through Olivia's veins. Yesterday at Garrison's Mercantile, she'd eagerly volunteered to accompany Kayla to the fashion show. But then her heart sank when she recalled Jake's words. He didn't think it would be a good idea. How could she say no to Kayla? It would break her heart.

Kayla's eyes filled with hope as she waited for an answer. Olivia couldn't disappoint her. She wanted to put an end to Missy's teasing once and for all. But was that the real reason? Or was it because it would give Olivia an opportunity to be a mother? Even if it was only for one night. "There's nothing more that I'd rather do."

* * *

"I'm going to run a few errands. Do you need anything?" Myrna tapped on the counter.

Jake peered from underneath Myrna's kitchen cabinet beside the sink. "I think I'm good, thanks. Are you sure it's nothing I can run out and get for you?"

Myrna snatched her purse off the island and flung it over her shoulder. "Not unless you're interested in getting your hair permed." Myrna scurried toward the door and turned around. "Olivia and I took Callie out earlier this morning to work with her, but she's still not back. Can you check on her? I know she didn't have breakfast. That girl doesn't eat enough. I don't know how she survives living alone in Miami."

"Sure, I'd be happy to check on them." Jake had hoped to see Olivia while he was working at Myrna's house. Lately, he couldn't stop thinking about her.

Myrna fumbled in her purse. Her keys dropped to the ground.

Jake approached as Myrna got on her knees and felt around on the floor.

"Here they are." Jake picked up the leather strap right in front of her. Myrna should have been able to see it. But maybe not. While researching online, he remembered reading about blind spots in the center of the vision of patients with macular degeneration. "Maybe I should take you to the hairdresser and whatever other errands you have to run? We can go out for lunch, too. I can finish installing these lights underneath the cabinets later."

Myrna stood and brushed her hands on her pants. "You sound like Olivia."

"What do you mean?" Jake asked.

Myrna released a heavy sigh. "Just because I didn't see my keys on the floor, you're ready to take away my driver's license and lock me up in the house."

Jake put his hands in the air. "Hey, wait a minute. Remember, I'm on your side to continue to live independently. That's why I'm trying to get Callie trained and doing all the upgrades around your house. I want you to maintain your freedom for as long as you can."

"I'm sorry. I didn't mean to sound so defensive. I appreciate everything you and Olivia are doing for me. Olivia cares about me and her motives come from her heart. Perhaps my actions don't reflect it, but I know my limitations and I don't plan on doing anything foolish. As difficult as it is for me to admit, I need help. I've reached out to my friends and I'll continue to do so."

Jake was coming to his own realization that Olivia's motives were coming from a place of love. Saturday night, after the twins' party, while Jake tucked Kayla into bed, he learned Kayla had asked Olivia to take her to the mother-daughter fashion show. Olivia had agreed, even though he had told her he didn't think it was a good idea. Initially, Jake had jumped to conclusions. Since Kayla had been so upset about the show, he believed she didn't really want to go. Perhaps Olivia had pressured his daughter. But after talking with Kayla, he learned his conclusions were way off base. Olivia knew how much the fashion show meant to Kayla. She understood what it felt like for a child to be left out because they'd lost a parent. "So what's got you upset?"

"Olivia's been struggling with Callie acting out. The pup basically goes bonkers when someone comes to the door or when a phone rings. I told her it takes time to train the animal, but being the perfectionist she is, she thinks if it hasn't happened yet, it won't."

Jake ran his hand through his hair. This wasn't good.

Myrna sighed. "Bless her heart. Even as a little girl, Olivia lacked patience. I remember one Christmas I took her to see Santa Claus at the local department store. When she saw the line snaking through the store, she told me she'd rather just write him a letter than wait. I can't help but think Olivia's patience is wearing thin with Callie because she's eager to return to Miami. And of course, when she leaves, she wants to take me with her." Myrna placed her hands over her stomach. "I know she believes she's doing what's best for me, but just the thought of moving makes my stomach sour."

Jake couldn't stand to see Myrna upset. He was upset, too. It would crush the twins if Myrna left. The town wouldn't be the same.

Myrna glanced at her watch. "I need to get going. I don't want to miss my hair appointment. Maybe when you go outside you can remind Olivia that training a dog doesn't happen overnight. Otherwise, I'm afraid she's going to pack my bags." Myrna turned on her heel and scurried out the door.

Jake cleared his tools from the kitchen counter. He'd have plenty of time to finish the lighting installation before camp started this afternoon. He grabbed his insulated cup and unscrewed the lid to top off his coffee before going out in search of Olivia.

Outside, the midmorning sky was overcast. With a 70 percent chance of rain in the forecast for later today, he'd have to set up a few things inside the barn in case he needed to move the camp inside.

Jake scanned the open field, but Olivia was

nowhere in sight. Off in the distance, he could hear Callie barking. Olivia must have taken her to the pond. He crested the hill and followed the grassy path that led to the benches Myrna's husband had built before he passed away. Jeb was handy with a hammer. He'd built the home where his wife still lived.

Jake squinted into the sunlight peeking through the clouds. He spotted Olivia sitting on the bench. She was leaning forward with her elbows resting on her thighs. Both hands covered her eyes.

Callie barked twice and came running toward him. Olivia didn't seem to notice the puppy was off her leash.

Jake scooped up the dog and moved closer to the bench. Olivia's shoulders quivered. She was crying.

He wasn't sure if she wanted to be alone to deal with whatever had her so upset. He didn't want to pry into her personal business, but he couldn't just leave her there.

Cautiously, Jake continued in Olivia's direction. He didn't want to startle her.

A gentle breeze blew and swept a tissue from Olivia's hand. She reached to pick it up, but Jake beat her to it. "Are you okay?"

She startled and quickly wiped her eyes on the back of her hand before pushing herself off the bench. "I didn't know you were here." Her brows rose as she looked at Callie. "Oh, I'm sorry. I was working with her and I got a phone call. I should have put her back on the leash before I took the call." Her arms dropped to her sides. "You're right. I'm not cut out to be a Puppy Raiser. I don't know what I'm doing."

"Hold on." Jake reached up with the tissue and blotted away the tears running down Olivia's cheeks. "I never said that. This is all new to you. It takes time. You're doing a great job with her."

"But I don't have time. I'll be thirty-six next month." Olivia flopped back down on the wooden seat.

Jake considered Olivia's words along with her actions. Something told him this wasn't only about training Callie. He took a seat next to her and put the puppy at his feet. "What does your birthday have to do with training Callie?"

Olivia shook her head. "It doesn't. I'm not talking about Callie."

Jake didn't want to pressure her, but it seemed like she was open to talking about what was bothering her. "I know you don't know me very well, but people tell me I'm a good listener. Maybe if you feel like talking about what's got you upset, I can help you."

"That's sweet of you, but I don't think anyone can help me."

"You'll never know unless you talk about it. Come on. I can't stand to see you like this," Jake said.

Olivia sat up straighter and pushed her shoulders back. She slowly turned to Jake. "My college roommate Beth called me. Mark, my ex-husband, got remarried last week."

"I'm sorry. I would imagine that's hard news to hear." Since Jake hadn't experienced a divorce, he couldn't imagine how this kind of turn of events would affect him. He always believed marriage was for life, but from what Olivia had shared, Mark had wanted out. *How do you stay with someone who no longer wants you?*

"It's not the marriage that surprises me. It's the rest of the story that—"

Olivia burst into tears again.

Callie perked up and jumped to her feet, releasing a cheerful bark.

Jake reached down and picked up the dog. He gently scratched her under the collar. "It's okay, girl."

Olivia sniffled and then shook her head, as if she wanted to shake out the last of her tears. "They are expecting a child."

Jake's stomach twisted. Unsure how to respond, he waited.

"I'm such a fool. Why did I ever marry him?"

This was unfamiliar territory, but he knew it was wrong for Olivia to blame herself. "You loved him. That's why you married him. Look, I don't know what happened, but I can tell you that Mark is the fool, not you."

Olivia rubbed her eyes. "Since we split, I kept telling myself it was all for the best. I wanted to have children, and he didn't. But that was all a lie. He wanted kids."

Jake's heart broke for Olivia. He couldn't imagine experiencing that kind of betrayal.

"He just didn't want to have them with me," she sobbed.

Jake squeezed his fists together. He'd never been the violent type, but if Mark was here, it would take every ounce of restraint not to punch the guy's lights out. Look what he'd done to Olivia, a beautiful and vibrant woman. But his actions had filled her with self-doubt. He placed Callie back on the ground and reached his arm around Olivia, not sure how she would respond.

Olivia slowly rested her head on Jake's shoulder. "Why did he stop loving me?"

Jake didn't know what to say. Olivia was only trying to process this devastating news. A part of him was glad he was there for her, yet a bigger part felt this was way too personal. The last thing he wanted to do was become invested in

Olivia's personal life. Eventually, she'd be leaving with or without Myrna.

"It's my fault. He didn't believe I could ever slow down long enough in my career to raise a family."

From what Myrna had told Jake, she didn't believe Olivia could, either. Although Myrna said she had prayed about it constantly, she thought Olivia believed giving up her career would disappoint her father. "Could you slow down? You invested a lot of time to become a doctor."

"If slowing down meant having a family, then yes, that's more important to me. After the divorce, I stopped taking extra shifts on my days off."

"That's a positive step in the right direction," Jake said. Maybe Mark and Myrna were too quick to judge Olivia.

"Having a family is something I've dreamed of since I was a little girl. It might sound silly to you."

Jake shook his head. "Dreams are never silly if they're what God has put into your heart. You should never give up on a dream."

A gust of wind blew, swirling the smell of honeysuckle in the air.

Jake glanced up at the sky. The clouds were thickening. "It looks like we might get some rain this afternoon."

"That's not good. I don't think Callie can afford to miss a class. I've been having a hard time with her."

"Myrna mentioned your recent challenges with Callie. I'll help you. She'll be fine. As for camp, it goes on—rain or shine."

Olivia flinched and pulled away. She'd been so upset maybe she hadn't realized how close they were sitting on the bench. "I'm sorry I dumped all this Mark stuff on you. That wasn't really fair."

"There's no need to apologize. I'm glad I was here to listen. I guess I'm returning the favor. You've been listening to Kayla a lot lately. I really appreciate it."

"Yeah, I've wanted to talk to you about that. I'm sorry if I was out of line when I accepted Kayla's invitation to the mother-daughter fashion show. I should have spoken with you first, but it broke my heart to see her so upset about Missy teasing her that when she asked, I couldn't say no." Olivia tucked her chin against her neck. "If you'd rather I didn't take her, I understand."

"Are you kidding? Ever since you agreed, she's been talking about it nonstop. If I told her she couldn't go, she'd never speak to me again." Jake smiled.

Olivia laughed. "I doubt that. She worships the ground you walk on."

"Well, my sources say you're high on her list of favorite people yourself," Jake stated.

Olivia smiled, and her face radiated. "I'd be dishonest if I said I didn't feel the same way about her—about both of your children. Getting to know them has been the greatest joy of my trip. I'm honored Kayla invited me to the show. I honestly can't think of anything I'd rather do—so thank you for allowing me to accompany your daughter."

Jake leaned in closer. "You know what?" He took both of her hands in his. "I think one day you're going to make a terrific mother."

Olivia took a deep breath. "Thank you, Jake."

Across the field, a black crow landed at the top of a pine tree and cawed.

"There is one thing I'm a little concerned about." Olivia squirmed on the seat. "Gammy has told me how people like to talk in Bluebell. I wouldn't want anyone in town to think—"

"What? That there's something going on between us?"

Olivia's cheeks blossomed into pink blotches. "Well, yes."

"It might shake things up a little around here." Jake wiggled his eyebrows. "Maybe a few people need to learn to keep their noses out of their neighbors' business."

Olivia poked her elbow into his arm. "Be nice. I think they all do it out of concern."

"Oh, look who's defending the small-town people now. I was joking, but you're right. We all take care of one another. That's the way it's always been."

Olivia gazed out into the open field and took a deep breath. "You know, the longer I'm here, I'm realizing that might not be such a bad thing."

Jake agreed. It was a great thing. Bluebell was the perfect place to settle down and raise a family. Once upon a time, his life had been proof of that. But he'd been there and done that. If Olivia changed her mind and stayed in Bluebell, could he take a chance on love for a second time? Or would his fears prevent any possibility of a future with Olivia?

Chapter Ten

"Good girl. You're doing great." Olivia dropped to her knees and kissed the top of Callie's head. She couldn't be prouder. The puppy's tail wagged back and forth as she devoured the attention.

All the credit went to Jake. He knew training Callie would require extra work and the skills Olivia didn't possess, but he went the extra mile. Despite his objection about her desire to move Gammy to Miami, he'd been generous with his time. Camp would end soon, but Jake planned to continue to work with Callie.

"It looks like she's finally got the Place command figured out," Jake said.

Olivia got to her feet and spun around in the open field. She spotted Jake approaching, dressed in faded jeans and a crisp white buttoned-up shirt. Despite the warm air temperature, goose bumps peppered her skin. His good looks were something she couldn't deny. Lately, they'd become more of a distraction. "I think you're right. Did you see her in camp today? Not only did she take her place on the mat without being told, but she stayed down, too. I felt like a proud mama."

Jake laughed. "You should be proud. You've worked hard with Callie."

"The extra time you've spent with us has helped. You're good at what you do."

"It helps when you love your work, but you probably know that."

Olivia believed practicing medicine was what she loved. She also believed it was what her father would have wanted. Had she been wrong? Honestly, she hadn't missed Miami and the stress of working long hours. She could never admit it to Gammy or to Jake, but Bluebell was part of the reason she had mixed feelings about returning home. "I don't think I love my work as much as you do. I used to, but sometimes seeing so much pain and death takes its toll."

Jake shook his head. "I don't know how you do it. I remember after Laura died, I wondered how the doctors dealt with death day in and day out."

"In our defense, sometimes we save lives or bring new life into the world." Olivia tried to convince herself that the good outweighed the bad, but she had the battle scars to prove that wasn't always the case.

"Daddy!" Kayla yelled as she and Kyle skipped across the field. "We finished putting away all the cones. Are you ready to go over to Miss Myrna's?"

"What's going on over there?" Jake asked.

"The church bake sale is this Sunday. We're going to help Miss Myrna bake snickerdoodles. I told you the other day." Kayla rolled her eyes.

Olivia's ears perked up. "That's right. I'm supposed to pick up some ground cinnamon on my way home today. I totally forgot."

"I guess it slipped my mind, too." Jake looked at Olivia and shrugged his shoulders.

Olivia picked up Callie. "I better get to the store."

"I need to pick up a couple of things from the store, too. Why don't I grab the cinnamon and you go ahead to Myrna's house?" Jake suggested.

"Can I ride with Dr. Olivia to Miss Myrna's house?" Kayla tugged on her father's arm.

Olivia nodded to Jake.

"We'll have to get the car seat loaded into Olivia's car first."

"We should buy Dr. Olivia a car seat since we'll be together a lot," Kayla suggested.

Olivia's heart warmed at the thought of a car filled with child seats. She forced the thought away. This was only temporary. Once she got back home to Florida, there would be no need for a child restraint system.

"It's only a trip to the grocery store, sweetie," Jake answered.

"But we'll be doing a lot of shopping for the mother-daughter fashion show, right, Dr. Olivia?"

Olivia willed herself to stop thinking about the future and enjoy the moment. "You're right. We have a lot of shopping to do. In fact, we might need to take a trip to Denver, if it's okay with your father."

"Yay! Can I, Daddy? Please! Please!" Kayla pleaded.

"Are you sure about this?" Jake asked.

"Of course. We can make a day out of it. We'll have lunch out, maybe get our nails done." Olivia rested her hand on Kayla's shoulder. "How does that sound?"

"Great! Maybe we'll run into mean ole Missy!"

Olivia and Jake shared a laugh as they headed to their vehicles.

Jake opened the back door of his truck and unfastened the car seat. "I'll just slip this into your back seat and we'll hit the road."

Kayla and Kyle raced to the cars.

"I'm going with Daddy!" Kyle announced.

"It's just us girls in your car, right?" Kayla looked at Olivia.

"That's right. Girls only." She winked.

"Okay then, we'll all meet up at Miss Myrna's house," Jake suggested.

Jake fastened Kayla into her seat. Then he and Kyle got into the truck and drove away.

"Come on, Dr. Olivia. Let's go," Kayla called out.

Olivia crated Callie and then climbed behind the wheel of the SUV. She settled against the leather seat and peered in the rearview mirror at Kayla. Her body shivered. This was what it felt like to have a family.

For the first five minutes of their trip to Gammy's house, Kayla chattered nonstop about the fashion show.

"When do you think we'll go shopping, Dr. Olivia?"

"Maybe next weekend, if your father says it's okay."

"Why do we have to wait so long? I wish we could go today." Kayla giggled.

"You have school. That always comes first," Olivia said.

"School ruins everything."

"Also, Callie's camp graduation is this Saturday. I'll need your help to get her ready." Olivia was looking forward to spending the day with the twins.

"But you and Daddy are still going to train her since she's a slow learner."

"That's true. Callie needs more work if she's going to help Gammy, but she's coming along." Olivia admired Jake for keeping his promise to his friend George. Thanks to Jake's dedication and additional training, she was confident Callie would meet her grandmother's needs.

"I heard Daddy tell Miss Myrna if Callie can't help her, you were going to leave and take Miss Myrna. Is that true?" Kayla's voice trembled.

Olivia tightened her grip on the wheel. The twins loved her grandmother as much as she did. "Try not to worry about it."

"Okay," Kayla answered.

Olivia relaxed her hands. Kayla appeared to accept her response, so she changed the subject. "If we get up early, we can get in a lot of shopping time. We'll each need to pick out two different outfits. One casual wear and the other something we can wear to church." Olivia loved that the clothing they planned to purchase would go to charity after the fashion show.

"Next weekend is so far away. I don't know if I can wait that long," Kayla said.

Olivia laughed. She remembered feeling the same. Now she wished she could stop the clock. "My daddy used to tell me not to wish my life away."

"What did he mean?"

"He wanted me to enjoy each day as it comes.

We never know what the future may hold. You'll realize when you get older the time goes quickly."

"Yeah, I guess he was right. Do you miss your daddy? I really miss my mommy. Even though Daddy tells us stories about her now, I feel like I'm forgetting her."

Olivia's biggest fear after her father passed was forgetting him. The sound of his voice, the touch of his hand, and how every night when he tucked her into bed he would tell her that to-morrow would be better than today. "Yes, I still miss him, but I learned the best way to keep him fresh in my memory was to talk to him."

"But how can I talk to my mommy when she's not here?" Kayla asked.

"You might not see her, but she's watching you. She knows everything you're doing. When you're upset, you can talk to her, just like you talk to God when you pray."

"Because Mommy is in Heaven?"

"Yes. And because of that, she'll always be with you. She's in your heart." Olivia spoke from experience. In times of difficulty, she often had chats with her dad.

"Can I ask you something else, Dr. Olivia?"

"I hope you know you can always ask me anything," Olivia answered.

"Is it bad for me to wish you were my new mommy?" Kayla's voice was barely a whisper.

Olivia was thankful for the stop sign because Kayla's question rocked her to her core, but it didn't come as a surprise. Two nights ago, she had dreamed the same, but it could never happen. It was wrong to give Kayla false hope. She took a deep breath and expelled. "Of course it's not. But it's important to remember I don't live in Bluebell. There will come a time when I have to return home."

Kayla remained silent. Olivia glanced in the rearview mirror and saw her rub her eyes. This was exactly what she was afraid of.

"Sweetie, are you okay?"

"Yeah." She nodded.

"Can you tell me what you're thinking?"

"I don't want the time to pass fast if it means you go away sooner."

It crushed Olivia to see Kayla's upbeat mood extinguished. "Why don't we follow my daddy's advice and enjoy each moment of every day?"

"Okay, but I'm still going to pray that you change your mind and stay."

Ten minutes later, Olivia navigated the SUV down the long driveway leading to Gammy's house. She filled the silence with music from an oldies station. Olivia always enjoyed listening to music from the 1950s. It surprised her to learn Kayla enjoyed the same. She said it was the station her mommy liked. "Okay, let's get inside and see what Gammy is up to. Your daddy and Kyle will be here soon and we can get started baking for the sale."

Olivia turned off the ignition and exited the vehicle. She opened the back door and reached in to unfasten Kayla's car seat.

Kayla wiggled out of the chair and jumped to the ground. "What's your favorite kind of cookie?" she asked as she took hold of Olivia's hand.

"Of course, Gammy always bakes the best snickerdoodles, but I've never told her that my favorite is oatmeal chocolate chip."

"Mine too! Do you think we can make those today?"

"I don't see why not. Gammy's pantry is well stocked, so I'm sure we can find some oats."

"Let's go inside and check," Kayla said.

They scaled the front steps. Olivia opened the screen door, and they moved inside.

"Miss Myrna! We're here," Kayla called out from the foyer.

The house was eerily silent. Olivia had seen Callie sniffing around in the side yard when they pulled into the driveway. "Gammy? Are you up there?" Olivia yelled from the bottom of the stairs.

"I'm in my bedroom," Gammy finally answered.

"Come on down so we can get started with the cookies. Jake and Kyle are on their way with the cinnamon."

"I need to wait a few minutes."

Something wasn't right. Her tone sounded weak. Olivia looked at Kayla. "Let's go check on her."

At the top of the steps, Olivia paused and sent up a silent prayer that Gammy was okay. They headed toward her bedroom at the end of the hall.

Olivia stepped inside. Gammy sat in her reading chair. She had her left foot propped up with a pillow on top of her footstool. In her right hand, she held an ice pack. "What's wrong?" Olivia raced to her side and dropped to her knees.

"It's nothing, dear." She fanned her hand in the air. "Go on and get started on the cookies. I'll be down in a minute."

"You never sit during the day except at mealtime. And even then, you're jumping up to do one thing or another."

Her grandmother laughed. "I just tripped, that's all."

"Where? Do I need to take you to the emergency room?" Olivia asked.

"Should I call my daddy?" Kayla cried out.

"You both sure have a lot of questions." Myrna rested her hand on Kayla's arm. "I'm fine."

"How can you sit there and say that? Tell me exactly what happened," Olivia demanded.

"My cell phone rang, so I was rushing from the family room into the kitchen. I tripped on the step. I shouldn't have been walking around in my socks."

Olivia released a heavy breath. That step was nothing but trouble. Her grandmother had no business living in a house with a sunken family room. "So you didn't see the step? Your eyes are getting worse."

"I just missed the step. I've done it thousands of times over the years, even when I was a lot younger."

Olivia wet her lips. "How did you get up here?"

"I just took it slow and exhibited a little determination." Myrna gave a dismissive glance. "Exactly the way your grandfather used to handle difficulties in life."

Olivia's fists tightened. Sometimes, her grandmother was as stubborn as a coffee stain on a white shirt. She would never admit to being in pain, her failing eyesight, or that this house couldn't accommodate her needs. It didn't matter how many changes Jake made—her gammy couldn't stay in this house. She took the melted ice bag from Gammy. "Kayla, stay here with Gammy while I go downstairs and get some fresh ice. Make sure she doesn't get up."

"I'm not a child, Olivia. I don't need someone watching me." Myrna attempted to stand, but winced in pain and dropped back into the chair.

Olivia stood and shook her head. "I'll be right back." She stormed from the room and rushed down the stairs, not sure who she was angrier with, Jake or herself. She shouldn't have made this agreement to train Callie. Obviously, the dog did not help prevent the fall. Olivia shuddered at the thought of how much worse it could have been.

Outside, car doors slammed. Jake and Kyle were home.

Olivia moved to the refrigerator and opened up the freezer. The icy blast of air did little to cool her temper. She needed to talk to Jake, but not in front of Kyle. The sooner she got her gammy moved to Miami, the safer she would be.

"Can you take this bag for me, son?"

Kyle reached for the grocery bag. Jake unloaded the other three bags from his truck.

Callie raced to the fence to greet them.

"Let's go inside and see what the girls are up to," Jake suggested.

Jake entered the kitchen and spotted Olivia wrestling with the ice maker. Her back was to the door. She murmured under her breath, but Jake couldn't quite make out what she was saying.

"I thought the place would smell of baked cookies by now," Jake announced.

Olivia jumped. "I didn't hear you come inside."

"Maybe it was because of the racket you were making with the ice maker. Is something wrong with it?" Jake moved a little closer and placed the grocery bags on the counter.

"Not the machine, but Gammy." Olivia slammed the freezer door closed.

Jake couldn't miss the anger washed across Olivia's face. He turned to Kyle. "Why don't you go find your sister?"

"She's upstairs in Gammy's bedroom," Olivia answered.

Kyle zipped out of the room.

Jake spotted the ice bag sitting on the counter. "What's going on?"

"Gammy fell and hurt her foot."

Jake's pulse ticked up. "You should have called me. Do we need to take her to the emergency room?"

Olivia picked up the ice pack and screwed the lid tighter. "She said she's fine, but I think she's only saying that because she knows I'm upset. She tripped on that stupid step from the family room into the kitchen."

Jake knew of the step. He had it on his list

of things to address. "I know that's an issue in this house."

Olivia placed her hands on her hips. "I don't see how it can be fixed without remodeling the entire family room area."

"Relax. We can install a ramp. It's not that big of a deal," Jake explained.

"Well, it sounds like another costly expense. You know my grandmother is on a fixed income."

"Myrna has been open with me about her finances. A couple of guys plan to do the job for free. This is a small town, remember? Your grandmother has done so much for this community, it's the least we could do for her. I know it's hard for you to understand, but we take care of each other in Bluebell."

"So you've said." Olivia shook her head. "I'm afraid that step is just one of many issues in this house. What about the fact that her bedroom is upstairs? Are you going to install an elevator or something?"

"Look, I don't have all the answers now. I'm doing the best I can to help your grandmother stay at her home. It's what she wants."

"I'm not sure Callie is the answer. She obviously wasn't there for Gammy today."

Jake raked his hand through his hair. "Of

course she wasn't. She's a puppy who's not fully trained. It takes time. It's what we agreed."

"Daddy, why are you fighting with Dr. Olivia?"

Jake spun around at the sound of Kayla's voice. "We're not fighting, sweetie." He glanced at Olivia, who simply shook her head.

Kayla shrugged her shoulders. "It sounded like it." She walked over to Olivia. "Miss Myrna wanted me to get the ice." Kayla took the bag.

"Thank you, Kayla. Tell Gammy I'll be up in a minute."

"Okay." Kayla raced out of the kitchen.

"I'm sorry. I didn't mean to pounce on you. I was upset about Gammy."

Jake understood Olivia's concern. She loved her grandmother. "You don't have to apologize. I know you're worried. Let's drop this for now. We agreed to help with the bake sale, so let's get the kids and have some fun."

"You're right. I'm going to run up and check on Gammy. I'll be right back with the kids." Olivia scurried out of the kitchen.

Jake slipped his cell phone from his back pocket and scrolled through his directory. He connected the call, but it went straight to voice mail. "George, hey, it's Jake. Remember that project I mentioned at Miss Myrna's house? Can you order the material this week? I'd like to get going on the ramp sooner rather than later. Call me when you have a chance."

Footsteps echoed down the front staircase. Jake moved to the cabinet that stocked all of Myrna's cookbooks.

"I don't know why you won't stay upstairs and keep the ice on your foot." Olivia guided her grandmother into the kitchen.

"I did ice it."

Olivia rolled her eyes. "For like two minutes."

"Ice, smice, I'm perfectly fine. I told you I just tripped. It was nothing. You worry too much, dear." Myrna walked toward Jake. "Hand me that cookbook. It's the one that has the biggest collection of cookie recipes."

Kayla moved close to Myrna. "Dr. Olivia said you probably have some oats in your pantry. She likes oatmeal chocolate chip cookies, too."

Just like Laura. Jake pulled the canister of oats from the bag and passed them to Olivia. "I bought these today."

"Thank you." She took the container and their fingers brushed. When their eyes connected, Jake noticed the pink hue that covered Olivia's cheeks before he pulled his eyes away.

Myrna slid a stool closer to the island and took a seat. "Okay, we've got a lot of baking to do. Olivia, did you pick up the cinnamon?"

"I got it," Jake answered and removed two bottles from the grocery sack.

"Perfect. We'll need at least eight dozen snickerdoodles to start. After we finish with those, you can bake the oatmeal chocolate chip. I also had a request for a few dozen peanut butter kiss cookies."

"We might be here all night." Jake rolled his eyes.

"That would be so cool!" Kyle cheered.

"Not when you have school in the morning, buddy. We better get cracking."

"Your father is right. Since I only have one oven, I think it's best that we each grab a mixing bowl and start making the batter." Myrna pointed to a stack of stainless steel bowls on the counter next to the sink. "Once the dough is ready, you can use these scoopers to make the balls." She passed a utensil to everyone. "I have more than enough cookie sheets, so we should be able to take one batch out and pop another into the oven. I've got the cooling racks lined up over there." She pointed to the counter on the other side of the kitchen.

"I feel like we just stepped inside Betty Crocker's kitchen," Jake joked.

"Who?" the twins asked in unison.

"Don't pay any attention to your father. He's just being silly." Myrna got up and scurried to the pantry. "Let me get everyone an apron so you don't mess up your clothes."

"Gammy, I wish you'd sit down and rest your foot."

"I've forgotten all about that. I wish you would too, Olivia. Really, I'm fine." Myrna passed a yellow apron to Olivia. "Here, put this on and get to work."

Olivia did as she was told. Jake locked eyes with her and smiled. Olivia moved to the empty counter space next to him. He leaned closer. "You better do as you're told or she might make you stay after class," he said with a laugh.

Three hours later, Myrna's kitchen smelled of sweet cinnamon and chocolate. Racks of cookies lined the countertop. A dusting of flour covered the floor.

"My hand is getting tired from stirring." Kayla dropped the wooden spoon into the cookie batter.

"Here, Kay. We can switch. I'm getting bored scooping the cookies off the baking sheet." Kyle extended his hand, offering the spatula.

Kayla snatched the kitchen tool and ran toward the cookies fresh out of the oven. She reached for the first tray. "Ouch! My hand!"

Jake jumped off his stool and ran to Kayla. "Did you touch the hot cookie sheet?"

"Yes. It burns!" Kayla cried out.

Olivia sprang into action. "I'll get my medical bag." She ran from the kitchen.

Jake heard Olivia's feet hit the wooden steps. A door slammed overhead. She was back in the kitchen in less than thirty seconds.

"Let me see." Olivia reached for Kayla's hand.

"Ow, it hurts."

"Right here?" Olivia pointed to the red mark.

"Yeah, it burns."

"I know it does, sweetie. I've got some gel in my bag. It will make it feel better."

"Will it stop the burning?"

"Yes, but first let's put your arm under some tepid water."

"Okay."

Olivia guided Kayla to the sink, turned on the faucet and gently placed her arm under the running water.

"Ouch!" Kayla cried out.

"I'm sorry, but I've got to get the area clean before I can put on the cooling gel. Are you okay?"

Kayla nodded and her lower lip quivered.

"You're being very brave. This is going to feel much better once I get the medicine on it."

"Okay." Kayla chewed on her lower lip.

Olivia squirted a dollop of the gel onto the burn. "Does that hurt?"

Kayla shook her head. "No. It feels kind of cold."

"That's how it's supposed to feel. That means the medicine is helping." Olivia continued to rub the ointment into Kayla's skin.

Jake stood close as Kayla's tears subsided.

Olivia placed the tube of medicine back inside her bag. She pulled out a bandage and unwrapped the packaging. "I'm going to cover the burn loosely with this bandage, okay?"

Kayla nodded and kept her eye on the wound.

"Now, you let me know if it hurts."

"Okay."

Olivia wrapped and taped the burn. "I'll send the medicine and bandages home with your daddy, so he can do the same before you go to bed tonight."

"Can't you do it later?" Kayla pleaded with Olivia.

"You'll be at your house and I'll be here looking after Gammy. I'll show your daddy how to doctor the burn just the way I did, okay?"

Kayla lunged from her stool and wrapped her arms around Olivia's neck. "Can't you come to our house? I only want you to do it."

Jake watched as Kayla squeezed Olivia tight, with no sign of letting go. His daughter's affection toward Olivia was both endearing and worrisome. The last thing he wanted was for Kayla to get too attached to Olivia. Her heading back to Florida soon would only leave a void in Kayla's life.

"Sweetie, come on now." Jake attempted to pry Kayla's arms from around Olivia, but she refused to let go.

Olivia looked up at Jake and shook her head, telling him it was okay. But was it?

"Thank you for taking care of me, Dr. Olivia. I wish you were my mommy." Kayla nuzzled her head into Olivia's shoulder.

Kyle sprang off his seat. "That would be so cool!"

Jake noticed Myrna's smile before she covered her mouth.

Kyle danced around the kitchen and glided toward Jake. "Why don't you marry Dr. Olivia? Then you won't be lonely anymore."

This was getting out of hand. Jake didn't doubt that Olivia was as uncomfortable with the direction of this conversation as he was.

Myrna clapped her hands. "Okay, now. Who's hungry?"

"We are!" the twins cried out.

"Who would like pizza?" Myrna called out to the group.

"We do, we do!" Kyle and Kayla cheered.

Myrna grabbed her purse off the counter. She removed her wallet and glanced at Jake. "Why don't you and Olivia run out to Mr. Pepperoni and pick up a couple pizzas for our dinner?" She passed her credit card across the island. "I'll call in the order."

"Pizza party!" Kyle jumped up and down doing a fist pump.

"You don't have to feed us dinner. I've got some leftovers from last night in the refrigerator."

"We don't want meat loaf again, Daddy. Pizza is much better," Kayla chimed in.

"Quit arguing with me. After all the help you all have given me, we're having pizza. Take my card. Olivia, you go along with Jake. The kids and I can finish the cookies."

Olivia grabbed her purse and looked at Jake. "You're wasting your breath."

"I know, I know. Shall we?" Jake motioned with his arm for Olivia to head out. He turned to Myrna. "Give them my cell number," he said.

Several minutes later, behind the wheel of his truck, Jake fiddled with the radio. "What kind of music do you like to listen to?"

Olivia pulled down the sun visor. "I like old-ies music."

Jake's heart squeezed. "That's what my wife used to listen to. She loved it."

"Kayla told me that was why she liked it, too. We were also talking more about our girls' trip to Denver. I'm sorry I didn't check with you first before I mentioned it in front of Kayla." Olivia tucked a piece of hair behind her ear. "I guess I got excited about the idea. It's been a long time since I had a day out with the girls."

"You don't need to apologize. I just hope Kayla didn't talk you into it. The fashion show might not be your thing."

Olivia ran her hands across the top of her jeans. "Actually, I'm excited about the show and spending time with Kayla."

"I know she's crazy about you." Jake hit the brake as the railroad crossing lights flashed.

"She certainly wasn't when I first got to town." Olivia laughed.

"True, but that's obviously changed. I hope she's not getting too used to having you around. I don't want her to get hurt when it's time for you to go home to Miami."

"I would never intentionally hurt Kayla. She's been through so much already."

"I'm sorry. I guess I worry too much."

"Kayla isn't the only one getting attached. Believe me, I've thought about how hard it will be for me to say goodbye."

"You could always stay in Bluebell." He hadn't meant to say that out loud. Or had he? He looked over at Olivia.

She examined her fingernails and turned her head.

They held each other's gaze.

Did she want to stay? If she did, it wouldn't be because of him. He was too old for her. There was too much baggage from his past. Yet the sparkle in her eyes told him *maybe*.

Excitement coursed through him and he leaned in.

Olivia followed his lead until their lips almost brushed, but then she glanced away.

"I can't. I'm sorry," Olivia said, turning away.

Heat filled his face. "No, I'm sorry. I don't know what I was thinking." Jake leaned back against the seat.

"I'm not sure what either of us was thinking." She pushed the hair away from her face.

Olivia broke the silence with a sigh. "Gammy is dropping hints for me to stay every chance she gets. During dinner last night, she even mentioned me becoming the town doctor. Luckily, she got a phone call and dropped that topic."

"There's been chatter about Dr. Dickerson retiring." Jake wasn't sure what would happen. Most doctors probably weren't interested in working in a small town where they might get paid with homemade apple pies. "We're hoping Doc hangs around a little longer. It's a long trip to Denver."

"There's no doctor's office closer?"

Jake shook his head. The train passed, and the gate lifted. He eased his foot on the accelerator. "Unfortunately, no. Doc tried to retire over a year ago, but he couldn't find anyone to take his place. His son, David, is also a doctor. We had hoped that he'd fill his dad's shoes upon retirement, but David went for the big bucks at a research hospital in California."

"I guess for some, it's all about the money."

After Jake lost his wife, he realized having money helped, but family and friends mattered the most. "Not you?"

"I'll admit, the money was nice as far as paying off all my student loans was concerned, but a few years into my career, I went to work in the ER. That position was what I'd worked so hard for. It was a lifelong dream finally realized. I make a real difference every day in the ER, and I think my father would be proud of me."

"So now you have your dream job?" Jake asked.

Olivia remained quiet and gazed out the window. "Have you ever wanted something so bad, or looked forward to an event, but when it finally happens, you're left feeling…?"

When Olivia couldn't find the right word, he took the lead. "Empty?"

"Yes. That's exactly how I feel." Olivia sighed.

Jake hit the turn signal and pulled in front of the local pizza parlor, Mr. Pepperoni. He turned off the engine and unfastened his seat belt. "I don't want to sound like I'm getting into your business, but maybe you're one of those people who prefers the race over the finish. I think that's common in goal-driven people."

"You might be right. After I finished my residency, I became obsessed with reaching my next goal. People who took time off were slackers. I volunteered to speak at seminars and covered coworkers' shifts. I did anything to keep my mind occupied. I worked nonstop."

"What were you avoiding? Or what *are* you avoiding?" Jake asked.

Olivia turned to Jake and unbuckled her seat belt. "What makes you think there's something I'm avoiding?"

"It's been my experience that people who fill every minute of their day with work are usually trying to avoid something or someone."

Olivia squirmed in the leather seat. "You're a wise man, Mr. Beckett. Are you speaking from experience?"

Jake laughed. "I think we all go through times where we bury ourselves in our work in order to cope with something we want to but can't control."

For a moment, silence filled the cab of the truck.

"Any advice on what to do when the person you're trying to avoid is yourself?" Olivia laughed half-heartedly.

"Maybe not advice, but like I said, I'm a good listener if you want to talk about anything on your mind."

Olivia looked at her watch. "What about the pizzas? I don't want to keep everyone waiting."

"Don't worry about that. Mario is always running behind on his orders. Besides, he'll send me a text when the order is ready for pickup. Tell me what's going on. Is this about your ex-husband and his expanding family?"

"I can't put all the blame on him. He spent years listening to my excuses about why I couldn't make it home for dinner. Or why I couldn't attend a function at his work. He put up with me for a lot longer than I would have."

"Why did you make excuses?" He hoped Olivia could trust him enough to share the burden she'd been carrying.

"After my father died, I blamed myself for his death."

Jake shook his head. "But why? You were only a little girl."

"I should have been there for him, but I wasn't. I know I can't change that, but I've lived my entire life trying to make up for my short-comings. Trying to make sure that I lived a life he would be proud of. I've done everything for him, and in doing so, I've lost the opportunity to have the one thing I've always wanted—a family of my own."

Silence hung in the air. There was nothing more Olivia wanted to share.

Jake's phone signaled an incoming text message. He checked the device resting on his console. "The pizza's ready."

"Great. I'm starving." Olivia opened the truck door and stepped from the vehicle.

Jake considered Olivia's words, and something struck him in his heart. The feelings for her that were growing in him needed to be pushed away. He wouldn't be responsible for denying her of her only dream. Olivia wanted kids, and on the day he lost his wife and child, he vowed never to have more children. The risk was too great. That chapter of his life had come to a heartbreaking close.

Chapter Eleven

"Thank you all for coming out today." Jake scanned the crowd and smiled. "The last day of camp is always bittersweet for me, but it's time for you and your puppies to spread your wings."

The crowd broke into cheers and applause.

Olivia reached down and picked up Callie. "Today's your day," she whispered in the puppy's ear before turning her attention back to Jake. It was becoming more difficult to not notice him, especially after their almost kiss in the car the other day. As much as Olivia didn't want to admit it, she wished the pizza had taken a little longer to bake.

"Today is a special day. It represents not only the culmination of all your hard work, dedication and love over these past several weeks, but also the beginning of your puppy's journey toward the opportunity to change someone's life.

There will be a lot of blood, sweat and tears ahead for each of you because raising a puppy isn't easy. It's downright hard sometimes, but trust me when I say the day you see your puppy helping its assigned handler, you'll forget those challenging times.

"Since Rebecca has the most experience with being a Puppy Raiser, she has volunteered to help with any concerns now that camp has concluded. If you have questions or problems, Rebecca and I will be available to support you either by phone, email or video conference. You'll never be alone, so don't forget that. After we eat, I want to get a photo of each of you with your puppy. Now Kayla and Kyle will pass out your certificate of completion while I go fire up the grill."

The class clapped and cheered, and shouts of "thank you" could be heard.

Jake handed Kyle and Kayla the folder with each participant's certification.

"My tummy doesn't feel good, Daddy," Kyle moaned.

"I can pass them out by myself." Kayla glanced at Kyle.

Olivia's ears perked up. Even though she wasn't working at the hospital, she was always on call. She moved closer to Kyle. "Does your tummy hurt or do you feel sick?"

"I don't know. It just feels funny."

"Can you show me where?" Olivia asked.

"Right here." Kyle held his belly button.

"Maybe you should go lie on the sofa for a while," Olivia suggested.

Jake felt his head. "He doesn't seem to have a fever. Maybe he's hungry. A piece of barbecue chicken or maybe a hamburger might make you feel better. He ate little at breakfast this morning."

Kyle wrinkled up his nose and shrugged his shoulders.

"Would you rather your sister take care of the certificates?"

"No, I want to." Kyle and Kayla left and headed toward the class.

Maybe Jake was right about Kyle just being hungry. She'd check on him later.

Jake packed his tablet inside his backpack and zipped it closed. "I guess I better get the grill started. Do you want to help me?"

"Of course. Just tell me what I can do," Olivia said.

"Myrna is up at the house getting some of the side dishes together, so that's covered." Jake flung his bag over his shoulder.

Gammy had left the house this morning while Olivia was still having her coffee. She said she had a list of things a mile long she wanted to do before the cookout. "Do you think I should go give her a hand?"

"You know your grandmother likes to take total control of the kitchen. Besides, I thought if we worked together, we'd get the food out quicker. We have a hungry crew here." Jake laughed. A light breeze blew a few strands of hair from Olivia's ponytail as they strolled toward the patio area.

"Watch your step." Jake reached for her hand as they climbed up the steep hill that led to an oversize brick patio. Once at the top, Jake let go of her hand. Olivia looked down and missed the feel of his large, calloused hand.

"Wow! This is quite a barbecue. It almost looks like you have a full kitchen." Olivia strolled toward the large barbecue with a brick base. The impressive design had a six-burner grill, a stainless steel refrigerator, a side burner and an abundant amount of counter space.

"This is incredible. It almost makes me want to take up cooking." Olivia opened the steel doors below the countertop and noticed a supply of plates, serving dishes and skewers.

"I built this a few years ago. My brothers and I like to have family cookouts in the summer months, so I thought I'd make it big enough for all of us to enjoy. Hopefully, our hectic schedules will slow down so we can plan something."

"You did a fantastic job. It looks like something you'd see in a home-and-garden magazine. I can't even have a small grill at my condo."

"Thanks. Another perk to living in the country, I guess." Jake scanned the property. "I'd like to do a bit more landscaping."

Olivia put her hands on her hips and looked out across the land. "With that incredible view of the Rockies, I don't think you need to do anything." She spotted an oversize swing situated underneath a massive Douglas fir. "I'm sure that's a beautiful place to watch the sunset."

Jake nodded. "It's one of the best views on the property. Maybe you'd like to check it out sometime?" Jake held her gaze.

Once again, their almost kiss came to mind, igniting a warmth on her face.

"Are you okay?" Jake asked. "Your cheeks look a little flushed."

Olivia placed a hand on the side of her face. "It must be this warm sun."

"Jake, dear," Gammy called from the open back door. "Do you want me to wrap up the corn on the cob in some tinfoil to throw on the grill? I've got all the hamburger patties ready to go. I still have to put the sauce on the chicken."

This was the perfect opportunity to put some space between her and Jake. The reaction Olivia had in his presence was becoming more confusing. "I'll come inside and help you." She turned to Jake. "If you want to get the grill started, I'll go bring out the food."

"That sounds good. Maybe I can throw some hamburgers and hot dogs on first, since they'll cook faster."

"I'll get them." Olivia turned on her heel and hurried into the house, unable to get the thought of watching the sunset with Jake out of her mind.

Two hours later, with everyone's stomach filled, Olivia stood alone in Jake's kitchen. Gammy and Kayla had gone to help Nellie with the inventory at the mercantile, so Olivia had volunteered to clean up while the guests played a game of horseshoes outside.

She walked toward the kitchen sink. The twins' drawings covering the refrigerator captured her attention. She'd seen them before, but a few more had been added. Her heart ached.

"Need some help?"

Olivia jumped, her fingers losing their grip on the top plate in the stack, and the porcelain dish crashed to the floor. "Oh, I'm sorry." She quickly set the other dishes on the counter so she could clean up the mess she'd created.

"No, it's totally my fault. I shouldn't have snuck up on you. It was obvious you were lost in thought." Jake moved toward the pantry, stepping over the broken dish. "Let me get the dustpan and broom. I'll have this cleaned up in no time."

Olivia picked up the remaining dishes from the counter and brought them to the sink. She turned on the water and began washing each by hand. Her thoughts stayed with the drawings on the refrigerator.

Jake swept up the remaining pieces, carried the dustpan out to the laundry room trash can and returned to the kitchen.

"What's on your mind?" Jake leaned in over her shoulder.

For the second time, Olivia flinched in surprise, but this time nothing shattered. She turned off the water and placed the plate into the drying rack. "What makes you ask?"

"When I walked in, you were a thousand miles away. Remember, I'm a good listener." Jake gently nudged his shoulder into hers.

Olivia took in a breath and moved to the refrigerator. "Can you tell me about some of these?" She pointed to the colorful drawings.

Jake followed her steps. He reached his hand toward the picture of a purple turkey. "I know the holiday is far off, but I found these when I was cleaning out my desk. They make me smile." Jake pointed to one of the drawings. "You're probably familiar with the traditional trace of your hand into a Thanksgiving turkey."

"I can take a wild guess who drew it—Kayla. She told me purple is her favorite color."

Jake nodded. "Even if it wasn't her favorite color, she would have picked something out of the ordinary. Kayla always likes to think outside the box, as noted by the red-and-yellow socks the turkey is wearing."

Olivia chuckled. "Unlike her brother." She pointed to the other turkey colored a rich brown.

"Kyle is exactly like his mother. She always followed the rules."

"What about this?" Olivia touched another drawing with a note written in the picture.

Jake rubbed his hand across his chin. "I remember that day like it was yesterday."

Olivia studied the attempt of a self-portrait created by Kyle. The boy in the drawing, dressed in a pair of denim overalls, stood with his hands behind his back and a tear streaming down his cheek. "What was he sorry for?"

"Kyle had gone fishing with his friend Zack and his father. They went to Mirror Lake, which is one of the largest in the area. Without my permission, Kyle took my pocket watch given to me by my father when I graduated from high school. It belonged to my grandfather. The watch didn't run, but my family had passed it down from many generations. My plan was to gift it to Kyle when he graduated. Unfortunately, it's somewhere at the bottom of the lake."

Olivia placed her hand to her mouth. "Poor Kyle. He must have felt so terrible."

"When Zack's father brought him home, Kyle was so upset he couldn't tell me what happened. He ran straight to his room and hid under the bed. I couldn't get him to come out. The bed didn't have enough clearance for me to go under after him, so I slept on top. Laura had passed a couple of months earlier. If she'd been alive, he would have gone straight to her. She always knew the right thing to say."

"So, when did he draw the picture for you?"

"I'm not exactly sure. When I got up the next morning, it was at my place on the kitchen table. He must have come out from underneath the bed in the middle of the night long enough to make the drawing, because when I woke up, he was still under the bed sleeping."

Olivia swallowed the lump in her throat. "That's the sweetest story I've ever heard." She tried to hold back the tears.

"Hey, don't cry." Jake reached for a napkin, tore it in half and gently blotted her eyes.

"You're blessed to have such wonderful children."

"I thank God every day for them. If it weren't for Kayla and Kyle, I don't think I'd have a purpose in this world."

Jake spoke the truth and didn't mean any

harm, but his words were like acid on her open wound. Had she wasted her life believing her purpose was to follow in her father's footsteps and be a successful ER doctor?

"Daddy, I don't feel good." Kyle entered the room. His face looked drawn and colorless.

Olivia cast her feelings away and raced to his side. She placed her hand on his forehead. "He's burning up."

"I've got to call Doc Dickerson." Jake slapped his hands against the back pockets of his jeans. "I must have left my phone outside by the barbecue."

"Here, you can search the internet for his number and use mine." Olivia grabbed the device off the counter.

"After Kayla's reoccurring bouts of strep throat last winter, I've got Doc Dickerson's number embedded in my brain." Jake stepped aside to make the call.

"Do you want to go lie down?" Olivia dropped to her knees, holding Kyle's hands.

"I feel like I'm going to—"

Before Kyle could finish his sentence, vomit projected onto Olivia's shirt.

"I'm sorry," Kyle whispered.

"It's okay, sweetie. Let's get you to the bathroom while your daddy calls the doctor."

Minutes later, Jake ran into the bathroom. "Doc is out of town on a family emergency."

"He doesn't have an on-call doctor who covers for him?" With Kyle in her arms, sitting on the bathroom floor, Olivia held the cool washcloth across his head.

Jake shook his head. "Only you." He knelt beside Kyle. "Are you feeling any better now that you threw up?"

Kyle nuzzled his face against Olivia's torso.

"I'd like to get him into his bed. I don't think he has much left in his stomach. Are you ready to go rest, sweetie?" Olivia asked.

Kyle flinched in her arms. "Ow!"

"What is it, son?"

"My tummy hurts."

"Can you show me where you feel the pain?" Olivia flung the cloth onto the vanity.

"Here." Kyle placed his hand against the lower right side of his abdomen.

"We need to get him to the hospital." Olivia rose to her feet with Kyle in her arms, careful not to alarm him.

"I don't want to go!" Kyle cried out.

"What do you think is wrong?" Jake's eyes widened.

"It could be his appendix. Has he ever had it removed?"

"No, but how can you tell?"

"The pain he experienced earlier was around his navel, but it's moved to his right side. Of course, I can't be sure without an ultrasound or CT scan."

"We'll have to take him to Denver. I'll go tell Logan what's going on. He can take over for me and wrap things up with the graduation festivities. I'll give Myrna a call, but I'd rather she not let Kayla know what's going on until we know anything for sure," Jake said.

"Good idea. Let me clean up my shirt a little and we'll get going." Olivia kissed the top of Kyle's forehead.

"I'll meet you outside in my truck." Jake sprinted out of the bathroom.

"I'm scared. I don't want to go," Kyle whimpered.

"There's nothing to be afraid of. You need to go to the hospital so the doctor can fix your tummy." Olivia brushed her hand across Kyle's cheek.

"But why can't you fix it?"

"Because the doctors at the hospital have everything they'll need to make you feel good again," Olivia reassured Kyle.

"But what if it hurts?"

"You'll be asleep, so you won't feel a thing. Then, when you wake up, your tummy will feel better."

"Will you be there when I wake up?" Kyle asked.

"I promise." Olivia took Kyle's hand and gave it a gentle squeeze.

"Okay, I'll go." Kyle rested his head on Olivia's shoulder.

With Kyle held tightly in her arms, Olivia raced outside to Jake's truck. The sound of birds chirping filled the air. She looked up and prayed silently to God that if Kyle was experiencing appendicitis, they'd make it to the hospital before the organ ruptured.

"I think I'm going to be sick again," Kyle moaned from the back seat.

Jake gripped the steering wheel and glanced in the rearview mirror, easing his foot off the accelerator as he navigated the two-lane mountain road.

"It's okay. I have this pan for you." Olivia held it underneath Kyle's chin.

Since Kyle first got sick, Olivia had been tending to his every need. She'd climbed in the back seat and held him close.

Kyle heaved, but nothing came up. He slumped against Olivia, and she reapplied the cloth to his forehead.

When Jake had explained to Logan they were taking Kyle to the hospital, his brother jumped into action. He'd taken the sodas from the cooler and loaded the icy water into Jake's truck, along with some washcloths. He'd thrown the pan into the back seat, which had come in handy three times since they'd left Jake's house.

Olivia continued to monitor Kyle's temperature.

"We should be at the hospital in about five minutes, buddy."

"I'm scared to go there, Daddy," Kyle whimpered from the back seat.

Jake's heart hurt for his son. What he wouldn't give to be the one in pain. "There's nothing to be frightened of. I'll be with you."

"But you were with Mommy and she never came home," Kyle cried.

This would be the first trip to the ER since he'd taken Laura that fateful night. Jake was afraid it would spark some memories for Kyle. It certainly had for him. He'd driven this route with the same sense of urgency. *Lord, please don't let it be the same outcome.*

"You're going to be just fine," Olivia reassured Kyle. "I promised you, remember?"

After what felt like an eternity, Jake spotted the entrance to the hospital and hit his turn signal. "We're here."

Two hours later, Jake sat in the familiar chapel where he'd prayed for his wife and son. This time, he prayed for Kyle.

By the time they'd arrived at the hospital, Kyle was in serious condition. Following a scan, the doctor came into the waiting room and delivered the news. If they'd been a few minutes later, Kyle's appendix would likely have ruptured. But thanks to Olivia's expertise, Kyle would be okay.

He should have never brushed aside Kyle's initial complaints of not feeling well.

"Would you like some coffee?"

Jake looked up. Olivia's smile warmed his heart. He rose to his feet and took her into his arms, not caring if he spilled the beverage all over himself. "Thank you."

"It's only coffee." Olivia laughed. "If you're not careful, it's going to end up all over your nice shirt."

He pulled back and reached for the cup. "Thank you for what you did for Kyle. If it wasn't for you—"

"Stop. It's nothing any trained doctor wouldn't have done."

Jake shook his head. "I brushed him off. He came to me because he didn't feel well and I told him it was only because he was hungry."

"You had no way of knowing at that point it could be something serious."

With their mother gone, Jake was his children's sole protector. It was his job, and he had failed. "But you knew. I don't want to even think what could have happened if you hadn't taken charge of the situation and realized what was going on with Kyle's stomach."

"Remember, I get paid to know when people are sick." Olivia rested her hand on Jake's arm. "Try not to be so hard on yourself."

Jake captured her gaze. "You were wonderful with Kyle. I know you're trained to treat people, but the way you were with him—the way he responded to you…"

"You're welcome." Olivia smiled, and they both took a seat.

Thoughts swirled in Jake's mind. Could he love again? Was he being unfair to his children by closing the door to the possibility of a relationship with another woman? With Olivia? It was obvious Kayla and Kyle adored her. Did she feel the same about them? About him?

For the next several minutes, they sat in silence.

Moments later, a sense of peace took hold. Jake hadn't felt like this in years. Was it because he knew Kyle would be okay? Or was Olivia opening his eyes to the opportunity of a new future?

Chapter Twelve

Olivia took a sip of her coffee and unfastened her seat belt. It had been a wonderful week. Thankfully, Kyle had fully recovered from the appendicitis and was back in school on Tuesday. Jake and his friends had completed work on the ramp in Gammy's sunken living room, along with a few other improvements. Olivia couldn't deny that with all the improvements, Gammy's house was probably now safer than her condo in Miami.

"Dr. Olivia!"

Kyle raced across the front lawn, wearing a smile from ear to ear. "Why are you just sitting there? Come inside. Daddy made pancakes."

Olivia's stomach grumbled at the mention of food. She'd gotten up early to take Callie for a long walk. Easing herself into the day wasn't something she was used to, but she had to admit, it felt great. "I hope he puts chocolate chips in them." She exited the vehicle, opened the back door for Callie, and the dog jumped to the ground.

"Sit," Olivia commanded. The puppy sat at her feet and looked up.

"Hey, she's listening." Kyle smiled.

Olivia laughed. It had taken a lot of hard work and determination, but she and Jake had turned the corner with Callie. Jake definitely was a pro.

"Yes, she is. Thanks to your father." Olivia ruffled the top of Kyle's head. "Let's get some pancakes. I'm starved."

Kyle ran ahead with Callie chasing behind.

Olivia smiled as she moved through Jake's house toward the kitchen. Family photos filled the tabletops and the wall going up the staircase. It was exactly what she dreamed of having for herself one day.

Outside the kitchen, she paused. Kayla was chattering nonstop about the day ahead. Jake laughed when she asked if she could get her fingernails painted purple. The banter between father and daughter was endearing. Jake was the type of father a woman would handpick for her children. But he'd closed the door on more children. What if he hadn't? Would things be different for them?

"Dr. Olivia!" Kayla's attention turned to Olivia. She jumped from the chair at the kitchen table and ran across the room. "I'm so glad you're here!" She wrapped her arms around Olivia's waist.

"I'm glad I'm here, too. I heard there are pancakes." Olivia took Kayla's hand and strolled toward the stove, where Jake stood with a spatula in one hand and the handle of the skillet in the other.

"Good morning." Jake smiled.

"Good morning to you." Olivia moved her head closer to the pan. "Those smell delicious."

Jake picked up the open bag of chocolate chips and poured them into the bowl of batter. "There's a slight wait on special orders." He winked.

Olivia's heart fluttered. Was it her imagination, or was Jake even more handsome this morning? "Word travels fast."

"Before Kyle took off upstairs, he told me you like chocolate chips in your pancakes. That's a favorite of mine too, but I don't make them often. I don't want to get the kids hooked on them."

Olivia crinkled her nose. "You're no fun. That was one of the best memories of my childhood."

"Pancakes?"

Olivia playfully nudged Jake's shoulder. "On Saturday mornings my mother always got her hair done, so my father was in charge of breakfast. He'd make us chocolate chip pancakes. He loved them, too."

"That's a wonderful memory."

Olivia nodded. No matter how much time passed, she still missed her father.

"Kayla, run upstairs and tell your brother breakfast is ready."

"Okay, but we have to eat fast. I want to have Dr. Olivia to myself for the whole day."

Olivia melted. She longed for the same.

Kayla ran out of the room and thundered up the hardwood steps.

"You might need a little extra sugar this morning if you want to keep up with Kayla." Jake poured another handful of chips into the bowl. "From the second her feet hit the floor this morning, all she's talked about is the shopping trip. I can't remember when I've seen her so excited."

"I think we'll have a wonderful time. I found a place to go for lunch where we can eat outside." Olivia had stayed up late last night scouring the internet for the perfect restaurant.

"She'll enjoy that. It's going to be a beautiful day. That's why I wanted you to bring Callie over. Kyle and I plan to take her out and about. It's good for her to continue to get more comfortable being around people in a public setting. She seems to enjoy the attention."

"I think you're right, but she has come a long way from our first solo outing." Olivia had taken Callie to the market, which turned out to be a disaster. After plowing into a few displays, she'd texted Jake for help. "I appreciate that. Some of the public spots in Florida might not be as welcoming to dogs as a small town like Bluebell."

Jake jerked his head toward Olivia. "So you've made your decision about moving Myrna? Does she know this?"

Her shoulders tensed. The last thing Olivia wanted to do was put a damper on her day out with Kayla. She hadn't decided. In fact, each day she spent in Bluebell made the thought of leaving more difficult. "I'm sorry. I shouldn't have brought it up. No definite plans. Let's not discuss that right now. Today is about Kayla... and pancakes."

Jake smiled and turned his attention back to the skillet. "I like the way you think."

"Look, Dr. Olivia! This is my size, and it looks just like the dress you bought for the fashion show." Kayla snatched the garment from the rack and held it under her chin.

The department store buzzed with activity.

Olivia scanned the store. She spotted several of what looked to be mothers and daughters spending a lazy Saturday afternoon shopping. Today was a dream come true, except Kayla wasn't her daughter. Was it fair to Kayla to pretend that she was?

"Maybe I should get this dress and we can be twins."

Joy welled up in Olivia's heart. She couldn't resist this vivacious little girl. "I think that's a wonderful idea. Let's go try it on."

A few minutes later, Kayla burst out of the dressing room door and twirled. "It fits me perfectly. Can I get it? Please! I want to look exactly like you and be exactly like you when I grow up."

The possibility of one day seeing Kayla all grown up, walking down the aisle to the man she planned to marry, was a glorious thought. But the truth stared her in the face. She'd be returning to Miami and leaving Jake and his family behind. Reality had followed her like a dark cloud over the past couple of weeks. No. She couldn't ruin Kayla's big day out. "Yes, we should definitely get it. I can't think of anything I'd like more than to be your twin." Olivia winked.

A smile spread across Kayla's face. She raced to Olivia and wrapped her arms around her midsection. "I wish this day could last forever."

Olivia's heart skipped a beat. She bit hard on her lower lip to fight back the tears. She, too, longed to hold on to this day for eternity. "That would be nice, wouldn't it? But remember, the day has just started, so there's a lot more shopping. Then, after lunch, we still have to go to Winston's and get our manicures."

"Oh yeah, I forgot!" Kayla jumped up and down.

"Do another spin and I'll get it on video."

"Yeah! We can send it to Daddy!"

"That's a great idea." Olivia removed her phone from her bag and hit the record button. "Perfect."

Kayla giggled and spun in circles, causing the dress to fan outward. She nearly lost her balance.

Olivia laughed and stopped recording. "Okay, go get changed back into your jeans and sweater and we'll pay for your dress."

"Okay." Kayla skipped back to the dressing room.

Olivia wrapped her arms around her waist. How could she ever say goodbye to this sweet child?

Seconds later, her phone vibrated in her hand. Her eyes narrowed on the screen at the text message. A weight settled on her heart. It was her supervisor. Olivia's mind raced. She hadn't given Lisa an exact date of when she planned to return to work at the hospital. If she responded to the text now, she'd tell her boss she was never coming back. Bluebell was where she belonged. Of course, she couldn't do that. She had to go back. Working as an ER doctor was her life. It was what her father would have wanted.

Olivia tapped the screen. Call me was all it said.

She crammed the device into her bag. Today wasn't the day to think about the stress and long hours that filled her days and nights working in the ER. She was having too much fun pretending to be Kayla's mother. Whether it was right or wrong, Olivia didn't care. At this moment, she was the happiest she'd been in a long time. Correction—ever.

Jake and Kyle strolled along the brick sidewalk in downtown Bluebell. Flower baskets bursting with purple petunias hung from the lampposts lining the street.

"Maybe we should take Callie into the library, Daddy. Miss Myrna goes there a lot."

"You're right. She volunteers there at least once a week." Jake patted his son's shoulder. "Good thinking."

Kyle looked up and smiled. "Do you think Dr. Olivia will change her mind and stay here?"

Lately, that question had caused Jake some restless nights. A part of him couldn't imagine Olivia no longer being a part of Bluebell, but he wanted her to be happy. "I don't know. I guess we'll have to wait and see."

"Can I ask you something?" Kyle chewed his lower lip.

"You know you can always ask me anything. What is it?"

"Is it wrong for me to want Dr. Olivia to be my mommy?"

Kyle's question was a punch in the gut. Jake could no longer deny the fact that he wanted the same. Lately, he envisioned what it would be like to share the daily activities of life with Olivia by his side. Even the possibility of Olivia being the mother of his future children had swirled in his mind. Day by day, his desire was outweighing his fears. How could he fault Kyle for his feelings when he was experiencing the same longing? "Of course it's not wrong."

"That's good because I think about it a lot." Kyle grinned.

"What do you say we pop into The Hummingbird Café and grab a German chocolate doughnut before hitting the library?" Jake definitely needed to change the subject.

Kyle's eyes widened. "Even though I had chocolate chip pancakes for breakfast?"

"Why not? Who says your sister and Dr. Olivia get to have all the fun today? Besides, Callie needs to learn how to be inside a restaurant and not beg for food. Right, Callie?" Jake looked down at the dog.

Callie barked.

"Let's go." Jake tugged on the leash as they headed to the café.

Minutes later, the threesome stepped inside the establishment. Jake removed his cowboy hat. His eyes zeroed in on the chalkboard covering the wall behind the cash register. Cowboy Chili was the special of the day. He loved that stuff.

Sally Raphine, the owner, waved and stepped out from behind the counter. "I had a feeling my special would bring you in today."

"Hi, Miss Sally!" Kyle waved back.

"Hello, Kyle." She reached down and scratched the top of Callie's head. "This must be Myrna's dog, Callie. She told me the puppy is quite the handful, but she sure is cute."

Jake was proud of Callie's progress. "It was slow going at first, but Callie has come a long way."

"That's good to hear. I certainly don't want Myrna being uprooted and moved to Florida." Sally pressed her wrinkled hand to her cheek. "This town wouldn't be the same without her."

Jake couldn't agree more. Myrna was a pillar in Bluebell.

"Should I put in two orders of chili?" Sally asked.

"As much as I'd love a bowl, we just popped in for a couple of to-go doughnuts. We're headed to the library," Jake said.

"Two German chocolates?"

"Thanks, Sally. Take your time." Jake scanned the tables and spotted Dr. Dickerson sitting alone with a cup of coffee. "We'll go say hi to Doc."

"Can I go outside to the ball pit?"

The side courtyard area had several picnic tables for outdoor dining, along with a play area. When they arrived at the café, they'd seen two of Kyle's friends romping among the balls. "Sure, but be careful."

"Thanks!" Kyle took off to the front entrance.

Jake led Callie across the floor. "Hey, Doc. Do you mind if we join you?"

"Please, have a seat, son." Deep crevices surrounded the doctor's eyes and mouth, evidence of a life filled with smiles.

"Sit, Callie." Jake tied the leash to the back of the chair before he took a seat.

The doctor tipped his head toward the dog. "It looks like you've done a good job with her."

"I can't take all the credit. Myrna's granddaughter and I have worked together to train Callie."

"I've seen you two together. You make a good team."

Jake smiled and his face warmed.

"Have you fallen in love with her?"

Jake froze. The doctor was never one to sugarcoat a situation. The chatter inside the café seemed muted, and Jake felt his face flush. He turned away from the doctor, but he couldn't escape the truth. He was in love with Olivia.

"Son, it's okay. I knew Laura all her life. I brought her into this world. She would want you to be happy."

Jake had been denying his feelings for weeks. A part of him felt invigorated to admit the truth to someone. "I know she would." He massaged the back of his neck. "But how do I move past feeling like I'm betraying her by falling in love with Olivia?"

"God wouldn't have brought Olivia into your life if He didn't know you were ready. He's shown you your future."

Jake brushed the tear that ran down his face.

Doc leaned across the table. "He created us to love. God doesn't want you to live the rest of your life grieving over a loss. He doesn't work like that."

The doctor pushed himself away from the

table and rose to his feet. He moved behind Jake's chair and placed his hand on Jake's shoulder for a second. Jake expected the doctor to say something more, but he remained quiet before he turned and strolled out of the café.

Was Doc Dickerson right? Had God brought Olivia to Bluebell to become his wife instead of moving Myrna to Florida? Had those butterflies and feelings of excitement over the past few weeks when he spent time with Olivia been part of God's plan? Jake blinked away the tears and closed his eyes. *I trust You.*

Chapter Thirteen

Olivia tipped her chin to the sun and relaxed her head against the back of the rocking chair. The curved legs slid her forward and backward while a soft breeze blew against her face. Gammy's front porch had become one of her favorite spots to share some quiet time with God. Something she could admit to neglecting back home. These daily moments of solitude had given her time to reflect and had provided her with clarity about what was best for Gammy.

The porch was also a perfect spot to relive every second of her shopping trip with Kayla. Four days had passed, yet she couldn't get the day out of her mind. She hadn't seen Kayla since dropping her off at the house on Saturday evening. Jake and his brother Logan had traveled south to pick up two Labrador puppies, so Kayla and Kyle were staying at Cody's house. Jake was due home today.

She traced her fingers over the top of her laptop. She'd brought it outside to read her work emails. Before last Saturday, she'd checked her emails regularly, but now they seemed like an intrusion—something that would only cause her stress and angst. By logging in to the hospital's secure site, she'd be transported from the idyllic world of Bluebell to a stark, clinical environment filled with fluorescent lighting and antiseptic smells that assaulted her senses. The constant beeping of the monitors served as a reminder of the high stakes involved in her work.

The screen door slammed behind her.

"There you are. I made a fresh pot of coffee. I thought you would like a cup." Gammy passed a steaming mug to Olivia.

The emails could wait. "Thank you. I had a cup of tea earlier, but the caffeine hasn't kicked in enough to motivate me to check my work emails."

Gammy swatted her hand. "You're still on vacation. You shouldn't be checking in with work."

Her time in Bluebell with Gammy, Jake and the twins had opened Olivia's eyes to how her struggle to separate work from her personal life had negatively impacted her marriage. She'd never quite put two and two together. Or perhaps she didn't want to admit it. But the reality was the reason she was single again and child-less at thirty-six was because she put work first. "My supervisor texted me the other day and I haven't gotten back to her."

"You've been busy. Besides, like I said, you're on vacation. She shouldn't be bothering you."

Olivia turned off her laptop.

"Oh, I almost forgot to tell you. Jake phoned earlier. He'd picked up the kids from school and was out running errands."

Olivia's pulse quickened. Lately, Jake, like Gammy, was occupying a lot of space in her mind. As much as she wanted to deny it, she'd fallen in love with him. But they were at different stages in life. She wanted children, and he had closed that chapter after he lost his wife.

"Jake wanted to know if we want to meet him and the kids at Charlie's Chuck Wagon in about an hour for dinner. I told him we'd love to. I figured you'd want to see him and the kids since it's been a few days."

Olivia was aware her grandmother wanted nothing more than to see her and Jake become a couple. "I think I can go a couple of days without seeing the Beckett family. Besides, soon I'll be returning to Miami and I won't see them again until I come back to visit you."

Gammy smiled. "Does that mean you're not taking me back to Florida with you?"

How could she do that to Gammy? If there was one thing she'd learned during her time in Bluebell, it was that her grandmother belonged in this town. Everyone loved her. Jake had proved his love and devotion to Gammy. He'd made her house a safer place and continued to train Callie. Olivia was at peace knowing Jake and the people in this town would watch over Gammy. "No, I'm leaving it up to you if you want to come and live with me. But I hope you'll remember my door will always be open for you and for Callie, even if your vision doesn't deteriorate."

"I appreciate that, dear." Gammy took a seat in the rocking chair next to Olivia. "It sounds like you've been doing a lot of thinking lately."

Olivia reached for her grandmother's hand and gave it a squeeze. "That's an understatement."

"I've been praying that you'll reconsider staying in Bluebell, maybe pursue a relationship with Jake. Is that something you've been thinking about?"

"Every day."

"And?"

"You know I can't do that." Her grandmother knew her better than anyone. Gammy understood why becoming a doctor was important to her.

"I had hoped you'd realize that life isn't all about work. It's about sharing special moments with family and friends. I don't want you to continue to spend your life trying to make up for something that was out of your control. You were a child. You couldn't have saved your father. I know you want to honor his memory and you believe working in the ER will keep you closer to him, but he would want you to have a family of your own and to be happy. I'm worried you're not truly happy with your life right now."

"But if I stay in Bluebell, I'll never have children of my own," Olivia argued. "Jake doesn't want to have more kids. I can't fault him for that after what he went through losing his wife and child. I love Kayla and Kyle and I know I could love them as my own, but I can't give up my desire to have my own children with the man I marry."

Gammy shook her head. "Jake would never ask you to give up your dream. I've seen you two together. I can tell you have feelings for each other, but unfortunately, you're both stubborn. You need to talk to him."

Olivia swallowed past the pain. "What's the point?"

"I've said my piece. If going back to Miami brings you happiness, that's what you should do. All I've ever wanted for you was to be happy.

But remember, working in a job that no longer gives you joy won't lead you to the life God has planned for you." Gammy smiled, then stood and made her way back toward the screen door.

Olivia considered her grandmother's words. As a child, she remembered her father talking about "God's plan." But had finding him unconscious on the floor been part of His plan? "I guess I should get cleaned up so we're not late for dinner."

Forty-five minutes later, Olivia spotted Jake and the kids—despite the dim lighting in the restaurant—sitting at a corner table. The aroma of grilled sirloin teased her taste buds. She was starving after skipping lunch to take Callie on a long walk.

"Dr. Olivia!" Kayla jumped from her chair.

"That child adores you," Gammy whispered in Olivia's ear as Kayla ran across the room.

"It seems like it's been forever since I've seen you. I missed you." Kayla wrapped her arms around Olivia's waist.

"I've missed you, too. Did you have fun with your uncle?"

"Yeah, Uncle Cody is funny." Kayla pulled on Olivia's hand. "I saved a chair for you next to me."

Olivia moved toward the table. Jake smiled

broadly as she approached. The sweater she'd carefully selected to wear this evening did nothing to prevent the chill of excitement that radiated through her body when she saw the twinkle in his eyes.

"It's good to see you both." Jake stood and helped Gammy into her chair before turning to Olivia. "Kayla saved a seat for you." He placed his hand on her lower back and guided her to the space beside his daughter. "I thought after dinner we could take a walk around the lake— just the two of us," he whispered in her ear before she sat down.

Olivia had noticed the lit path that circled the lake when she and Gammy arrived. The idea of walking it with Jake hadn't crossed her mind, but it sounded more appealing than that sirloin steak she'd been craving. "I'd like that," she whispered back.

After their meal, the server cleared away the plates. While they waited for dessert, the children went to the jukebox with a handful of quarters.

Gammy cleared her throat. "Well, if you don't tell him, I guess I will."

Olivia wasn't sure what Gammy was referring to, so she complied. "Go right ahead."

"My granddaughter has decided that after all of your renovations and dog training, I'm safe to stay in Bluebell on my own."

Olivia's heart plummeted to the bottom of her stomach. Although it had been her decision, hearing it spoken out loud made it permanent.

Jake clapped his hands. "That's the best news I've heard all week. So you'll be staying on as well?"

Was that a hint of hopefulness Olivia detected in Jake's voice? "No, but I'm sure I'll be back for visits." Would she? Or would she get pulled back into the endless cycle of late-night shifts that left her too exhausted to do anything but sleep? Her phone chimed inside her purse.

"I've been hearing that phone ring all evening, dear. Don't you think you better check?" Gammy suggested.

"I didn't want to be rude."

Jake shrugged his shoulders. "I don't mind. Go ahead."

Olivia grabbed her bag from where it was hanging on the back of her chair and fished out her phone. She tapped the device and opened the text message. Her eyes opened wide and her hand trembled. The room felt as if it were spinning.

"What is it, dear? What's wrong?" Gammy asked.

Jake leaned in closer. "You okay?"

For the second time, Olivia read the incoming text message from her supervisor to make sure she'd read it correctly. Her mind reeled. Since she'd first arrived in Bluebell, all she could think about was how to convince Gammy to move back to Miami. She wanted no attachments with anyone in the community, particularly Jake and his adorable children. Now the last thing she wanted to do was leave, but what choice did she have? She'd lose her job if she didn't return. But it wasn't just a job for Olivia. If she wasn't practicing medicine, she'd lose the only connection to her father she had left. Her chair screeched as she forced herself away from the table and ran toward the front door, ignoring the calls from Gammy and Jake.

Once outside, Olivia raced to the lake. She sprinted down the path until she was out of breath. She stumbled to a bench and collapsed. Why was this happening? Why was she being forced to choose? It wasn't fair. Again, she scanned the screen to triple check, but she hadn't been mistaken. Her supervisor had booked her on the first available flight late tomorrow evening, which meant she would miss the mother-daughter fashion show. Either she would be on that flight or she'd have no job to go home to.

Jake nearly fell on his face when his foot stumbled over a rock. He didn't care. Finding Olivia was all he cared about. The look on her face when she'd read the text message terrified him. Regaining his footing, he picked up his pace and headed farther down the path. Thoughts raced through his mind. Was the message from her ex-husband? Whoever it was from owed Olivia an apology.

Finally, he spotted her sitting on one of several benches circling the lake. It was a good thing because he wasn't sure he could run much farther. Slowing his steps, he approached with caution. "Are you okay?"

Olivia had her face buried in her hands.

Jake sat down and waited for her to speak. He'd wait all night if need be. Shoot, he'd wait forever. He loved her.

Olivia lifted her head and cleared her throat. "The text was from my supervisor. There's a major staff shortage at the hospital because of the flu. She's booked me on the next flight back to Miami."

His stomach dropped. "When?"

Tears streamed down her face. "Tomorrow evening."

"What about Kayla? The fashion show is on Friday. You promised her." He squeezed his fists tight. Every muscle in his body tensed. He'd known this would happen, yet he'd done nothing to prevent the relationship between Olivia and

Kayla from growing. Now his baby would have her heart broken, exactly like he'd predicted.

"Don't you think I know that? I've been looking forward to it as much as Kayla."

Jake shook his head. "That doesn't matter. She's a child. She won't understand why you have to go, only that you're leaving her."

"It's my job, Jake. I don't know what I can do."

"Can't you ask for your return to be delayed a couple more days?"

"I've ignored her emails, texts and phone calls for the past week. She's not cutting me any slack. It's tomorrow or I won't have a job."

Jake raked his fingers through his hair. How would he tell Kayla?

Olivia inched off the bench. "I'll talk to Kayla. Maybe Gammy can take her in my place."

"No!" Jake grabbed her hand. "I don't think you understand how much this means to Kayla."

"How can you say that? I've walked in her shoes. Growing up without a father, I missed out on countless special events. I know exactly what she's going through." Olivia wiped the tears from her face. "Please don't say I don't understand. That's not fair."

Jake forced his shoulders to relax. He was being too hard on Olivia. It wasn't all her fault.

"I'm sorry. I know you understand. My protective instincts are getting the best of me, I suppose. I just hate to see her disappointed. She's been looking forward to the show since you agreed to go with her." Jake couldn't forget the look on her face when she'd come home from their shopping trip last weekend. Kayla had talked nonstop about their matching outfits. Olivia leaving before the fashion show would crush her.

"If there was any way I could stay until Friday, I would, but I can't risk losing my job."

Jake nodded. "Let's go back inside and have our dessert. But don't mention this to Kayla."

"Don't you think I should be the one to tell her?"

"No. I'll talk to her when we get home. It will be better if it comes from me."

Olivia rubbed her arms. "Can't I even say goodbye to her and Kyle?"

"No, I think it's best if you just leave. Let me handle everything." Jake pushed himself off the bench. "We better go back inside."

A couple of minutes later, Jake and Olivia rejoined Myrna at the table. Thankfully, the children were at the indoor play area.

"What's going on?" Myrna asked. She looked at Olivia. "Have you been crying?"

Jake leaned back in his chair while Olivia explained the situation to her grandmother.

"You can't leave!" Myrna's brows furrowed. "Kayla will be heartbroken."

"I explained everything to Jake, Gammy. I don't have a choice. If I don't go back on Thursday night, I won't have a job."

"Would that be the end of the world?"

Olivia looked over her shoulder. "We shouldn't be talking about this now. Jake wants to tell Kayla I'm leaving after they get home."

Myrna released a heavy breath and shook her head. "I don't agree with any of this, but for Kayla's sake, I'm going to stay out of it. I hope you both know what you're doing."

The table remained quiet for the next five minutes until Kyle and Kayla returned.

"What's for dessert?" Kyle asked, breaking the silence.

"I want a piece of chocolate cake," Kayla announced. "You should try it, Dr. Olivia. It's the best."

Jake waited for Olivia to respond, but she simply forced a smile. Myrna tossed him a look of concern.

"What's going on?" Kyle looked at the adults. "Why's everyone acting funny? Did you ask Dr. Olivia on the date?"

Jake flinched and Kyle's eyes widened.

"I'm sorry, Daddy. I forgot it was a secret." Kyle covered his mouth.

Kayla bounced in her seat. "What secret?"

Her brother dropped his hand away from his mouth. "Daddy likes Dr. Olivia. Last night when he tucked me in, he told me he was going to ask her on a date."

"Kyle!" Jake shouted loud enough for the neighboring table to glance their way. "Sorry." He waved a hand.

"Cool!" Kayla voiced her opinion.

Myrna laughed out loud. "I love it."

Olivia's face turned red.

Jake could do nothing but shake his head.

Later that evening, Jake sat hunched at the kitchen table with a cup of coffee between his hands. The pitter-patter of feet vibrated overhead as the children scurried around getting ready for bed. The entire trip home from the restaurant, Kayla had talked about the fashion show. He dreaded telling her that Olivia wouldn't be taking her, but at least she could go with Myrna. After dessert, Myrna had pulled Jake aside and offered to accompany Kayla to the show. Jake appreciated her kind gesture, but he knew in his heart Kayla only wanted Olivia.

Since learning Olivia was leaving, Jake had wrestled with his emotions. Should he have made his feelings toward her known when he'd found her down by the lake? Would that have affected her decision to leave? It was too late now. She planned to leave.

"Daddy, we're ready to be tucked in," Kayla called from the top of the stairs.

Jake sent up a silent prayer, asking for the words to come before he headed upstairs.

After Kyle said his prayers, Jake moved down the hall to Kayla's room. Before entering, he could hear his daughter telling her stuffed bulldog, Rocky, all about her trip to Denver with Olivia and the upcoming fashion show.

"Hey, sweetie. Are you ready to say your prayers?"

Kayla nodded and tucked Rocky under the pink comforter. Midway through her prayers, she yawned before saying "Amen."

Jake kissed the top of her head. "I need to talk to you for a minute about the fashion show."

Kayla's sleepy eyes lit up. "I can't wait!"

"Well, there's been a slight change of plans."

Kayla's brow crinkled.

"You'll still be going, but Miss Myrna will take you instead of Dr. Olivia."

Kayla pushed the comforter aside and popped upright in the bed. "Why? Did something happen to Dr. Olivia? Did she go to Heaven like Mommy did?" Her face turned pale.

Jake placed his hands on her shoulders to settle her down. "No, don't worry. She's fine."

"Then why isn't she taking me? She promised." Tears spilled down her face as she burrowed back under the comforter.

"She really wanted to, but she has to go back to work. Remember, she has a very important job. She helps sick people get well at the hospital, but right now, they don't have enough doctors, so she has to go back to help."

Kayla appeared lifeless in the bed.

Jake gently brushed her hair away from her face. "She'd stay if she could. I know she cares a lot for you."

"Then how could she go? I thought she was going to be my new mommy." She turned onto her side. "Leave me alone," she said and buried her face in the pillow and cried.

Jake reached over and turned off the princess lamp on the nightstand. "Tomorrow will be better, sweetie," he whispered. "I promise."

Chapter Fourteen

Thursday morning, Olivia took a deep breath and tucked the last sweater into her suitcase. She'd been awake since three o'clock. Tossing and turning, she'd spent a restless night in bed, knowing it would be her last sleep in Bluebell.

At first light, she'd peeled herself out from under the down duvet and thrown on a pair of yoga pants, a sweatshirt and tennis shoes to take Callie for a long walk. Once home, Gammy made her applesauce pancakes with warm maple syrup. Olivia would miss her grandmother and Callie after she returned to Miami, but she was confident Gammy belonged in Bluebell.

One thing she wasn't confident about was leaving Jake and the twins. Olivia had picked up the phone to call Jake many times since last night. She wanted to share her heart and tell him she'd fallen in love with him—that she could sacrifice her desire to have children of her own, if it meant she could be with him and his children. But what was the point? After breaking his daughter's heart, he'd probably never want to speak with her again. She couldn't blame him.

"Lunch is ready," Gammy called from downstairs.

Olivia sighed. She placed the last pair of pants into the luggage and zipped it closed. Her time in Bluebell had come to a close. It was time to get back to reality.

Once downstairs, she placed her suitcase next to the front door. Moving to the kitchen, she stopped short just outside the entrance, taking in the sounds of Gammy busying herself as she made their last meal together for a while. The familiar sounds of clanking pots and pans were as soothing as a dollop of honey in a cup of freshly steeped tea.

Olivia's senses were aware of all that surrounded her. She wanted to remember everything about this place, hoping it would provide comfort once she was back home and alone in her condo. The aroma of Gammy's fried chicken caused her stomach to rumble and drew her into the kitchen.

"Are you hungry?" Gammy turned the burner off and moved the skillet onto the trivet. Her normally cheerful smile was noticeably absent.

"I am now. The chicken smells delicious. You shouldn't have gone to all this trouble. I could grab something to eat at the airport."

Gammy swatted her hand. "This is no trouble. It's what I do."

It certainly was. Her grandmother was the most selfless person she'd ever known.

The doorbell rang. Callie took off running to greet the visitor.

"Grab a plate. I'll get the door." Gammy untied her apron and flung it on the counter.

Muted conversation carried through the foyer until Dr. Dickerson entered the kitchen.

"Hello, Olivia." The elderly gentleman nodded and rubbed his right knuckles with his left hand. "My arthritis is acting up. There must be rain in the forecast."

Olivia extended her hand. "I think I heard something about storms. It's good to see you, Doctor. Did you smell the chicken from town?"

He ran his palm in a circular motion over his stomach. "It's my favorite. I always told Myrna she should have opened a restaurant. She'd have customers from all over the state."

"Well, there's plenty for everyone, so please sit down and I'll bring the food to the table." Gammy smiled, happy to be serving a meal.

With the plates filled, Gammy took her seat

across from the doctor. "What brings you by, besides my fried chicken?"

Dr. Dickerson picked up his napkin and wiped his mouth. "Well, after months of going back and forth, I'm finally taking your advice, Myrna. I plan to retire next month."

Gammy's eyes lit up. "That's wonderful. I'm sure Doris is thrilled."

"She's already planning our first cruise. She reminded me we haven't taken a vacation in over twenty years."

Olivia admired his dedication to the town. "Congratulations. I'm happy for you and Doris. Did you find someone to take over your practice?" Olivia would hate to see the town without a doctor. When Kyle got ill, she experienced firsthand how stressful it was to travel a long distance when a loved one was sick.

"Actually, that's why I'm here." Dr. Dickerson took a deep breath and continued. "I hope I can convince you to take over the practice. Apart from the necessary licensing requirements, you could step in without missing a beat. I've spoken to many people around town and everyone is in full agreement. You are the best person for the job."

Gammy clapped her hands together. "Wonderful!"

Stunned by the offer, Olivia was tongue-tied.

The idea of staying in Bluebell and being a part of such a wonderful community was appealing, but the reality was she belonged in Miami. It was what her father would have wanted for her. Besides, given her feelings toward Jake, living in the same town with him and the twins would be too painful. "I'm flattered by the offer. Truly, I am."

"I detect some reservation." The doctor's smile slipped from his face.

"I'm grateful for my time in Bluebell, but Miami is my home. The ER needs me, especially now with the doctor shortage." Olivia glanced at Gammy, who discreetly wiped a tear from her cheek.

"I can't say that I'm not disappointed, but I respect your commitment to your position and your colleagues," Dr. Dickerson said. "I'm sure the hospital appreciates your dedication."

A casual conversation carried them through the rest of their meal. The excitement over the upcoming retirement that earlier filled the air had faded.

Thirty minutes later, Dr. Dickerson left and Olivia and Gammy cleaned up the kitchen in silence.

"I think I'll head out to pick up my outfits for the fashion show." Myrna approached Olivia with open arms. "It's probably best if I'm not here when you leave. It's too sad."

Olivia moved forward and the women embraced.

"I'm going to miss you bossing me around. You know that, don't you?" Olivia joked.

"It's only because I love you so much."

Olivia took a deep breath. "I love you, too."

"I know you have to do what's best for you. I admire your strength, dear. You're so much like your father." Myrna drew back and narrowed her eyes at Olivia. "I hope you realize how proud he would be of you."

Olivia buried her face in Gammy's shoulder and hugged her tighter. A part of her didn't want to let go or decline the doctor's offer. But she had to face the reality. There was no future for her and Jake.

Following a few seconds of silence, Myrna pulled away and wiped her eyes. "I better go."

Olivia was grateful when Gammy volunteered to take Kayla to the mother-daughter fashion show. Hopefully, her presence would ease Kayla's disappointment. "I don't like the idea of you driving to Denver alone."

"I won't be going by myself, dear. I'm heading over to Ruth's house. She will be driving, so you don't have to worry." She moved across the kitchen to the sink.

Olivia stepped closer to the kitchen sink. "Will you email me photos of the show?"

"Of course."

Olivia hugged her grandmother one more time. "Please drive safe."

"I always do." Gammy grabbed her purse from the pantry and headed out the door.

Moments later, Olivia heard Gammy's car start and drive away.

A chill caused Olivia to shiver as she stood alone in the kitchen. Her eyes scanned the room, taking in every sight and smell to carry back to Florida. She inhaled one last deep breath before heading out to the airport. It was time for Olivia to go home.

"Maybe you should call her?" Logan opened the crate, and Buddy, the German shepherd puppy, cut loose across the field as if chasing a rabbit.

"Who?" Jake glanced in his brother's direction.

"You're kidding, right? Come on. You've been moping around all day." Logan shook his head and mumbled as he headed toward the barn. "You better go after her, man. God has given you a second chance—don't blow it."

His brother knew him well. Despite his best efforts, Jake hadn't been able to stop thinking about Olivia. Last night, he'd searched her flight information multiple times. Her plane left on time and landed safely. In between checking her flight status, he'd been consoling the kids and trying to explain why Olivia had to go back to Miami. The rest of the evening, he'd questioned whether he'd made the biggest mistake of his life by not telling her he was in love with her and wanted nothing more than to raise a family together.

Jake glanced at his watch as he headed toward the house. A sky of restless clouds drifted overhead. Myrna had phoned this morning to let him know she planned to meet the kids' school bus and help them with their homework, but he wanted to be there when they walked in the door.

Myrna was doing everything in her power to keep their minds occupied and off Olivia. Jake had tried his best to stay upbeat, but he missed Olivia, too. There was a giant hole inside him he couldn't seem to fill. Even working to train his latest service dogs couldn't fill the emptiness. Hopefully, once the mother-daughter fashion show was behind them, Kayla would get past the void left in her life by Olivia's departure. But the question was, would he?

He reached the back patio and his eyes focused on the swing between the Douglas firs.

I'm sure that's a beautiful place to watch the sunset. Olivia's words played in his head and he kicked his boot into the ground. Because of his stubborn ways, they wouldn't share a sunset together.

He scanned the property and listened to a song sparrow trill in the distance. Olivia was right—there was nothing more the land needed. Except, in Jake's opinion, it needed her presence.

"Daddy! Kayla locked herself in her bedroom and she won't come out," Kyle shouted from somewhere in the house. Jake wiped his boots on the laundry room rug and took a deep breath. *Lord, give me strength.*

He scaled the stairs and found Myrna and Kyle outside Kayla's bedroom door. "What's going on?"

Myrna spoke first. "It seems Missy is at it again." She rolled her eyes.

Jake's busy schedule hadn't given him time to call Missy's parents. Now he wished he'd made it a priority. "Do you know what happened?"

"She's so mean!" Kyle wasted no time in reporting the story. "We were in the lunchroom and she came to our table. She started teasing Kayla about the fashion show."

Of course. That seemed to be the hot topic lately. Jake just wanted the show to be over. "What did she say?"

"She said it wasn't a grandmother-and-grand-daughter fashion show, so Kayla and Miss Myrna shouldn't be in it. She said…" Kyle paused and looked down at the floor.

"What is it, son? You can say it." Jake glanced at Myrna.

"She said Miss Myrna was too old to be a model." Kyle turned to Myrna. "Sorry."

Myrna straightened her shoulders. "It's not your fault, Kyle."

Jake didn't have a good feeling about this evening. His instincts told him to keep Kayla home. Why subject her to more ridicule by Missy? But what would that teach his daughter? Jake's father always taught him to never give the power to a bully. The best way for Kayla to handle someone like Missy was to stand up to her. Easy for him to say. "I'll talk to her." He knocked on her door and waited for a response. When she didn't answer, he knocked again. "Kayla, can you open the door?"

"Go away!"

Myrna's and Kyle's eyes darted in Jake's direction.

"Why don't you and Kyle go down to the kitchen? Kyle is probably ready for his snack."

Myrna nodded to Jake. "Let's go, hon. I brought over some fresh chocolate chip brownies."

Jake waited until they were downstairs. He

reached up over the door frame and grabbed the key to Kayla's room. Slipping the key into the hole, he slowly turned the knob. "I'm coming in." He paused before entering.

Jake's heart sank when he spotted his daughter sitting at her desk. Kayla gazed at the portrait of her mother he'd had professionally matted and framed for Kayla's birthday last year, after she'd told him it was her favorite photograph of her mother.

He slowly approached the desk and placed his hand on Kayla's shoulder. "Can you tell me what happened, sweetie?"

Kayla sprang from the chair and threw her arms around Jake's waist. Without hesitation, he scooped her up. He couldn't recall when she'd ever held on so tight. She buried her face in his shoulder and cried.

"Oh, baby, I'm so sorry." He carried her across the room and sat down on the edge of her bed. When would it ever get easier? Jake had always considered himself a problem solver. There was nothing he couldn't fix when he put his mind to it. But raising a little girl on his own was more than he could handle. Even with Myrna's help, he felt like he was failing his daughter.

Finally, Kayla's body stopped quivering, and her tears subsided. She lifted her head off his shoulder and looked him in the eye. "I'm sorry I locked my door. I know I'm not supposed to."

"It's okay. I understand you wanted to be alone, but sometimes it's good to talk to someone when you're upset."

Kayla nodded. "That's what Dr. Olivia told me. She said keeping stuff inside makes you feel worse."

Jake missed Olivia's words of wisdom. He missed a lot of things about her. "She was right. So, are you ready to talk?"

Kayla pushed her hair off her face and wiped her eyes. "Do I have to go to the fashion show?"

Jake studied his daughter. "Not if you don't want to."

Frowning, she chewed her lower lip. "Does that make me a scaredy-cat?"

Jake flinched. "Who called you that?"

"Kyle said if I didn't go, Missy would start calling me a scaredy-cat."

"What do you think?"

Kayla's forehead crinkled. "Well, if I go, she can't call me that."

"That's true." Jake nodded.

"What do you think Dr. Olivia would do?" Kayla studied his face.

"I think Dr. Olivia would probably go with Miss Myrna and have the best time that she could. She wouldn't allow Missy or anyone else to steal her joy."

Downstairs, the doorbell chimed.

Kayla hugged Jake and jumped off his lap. "Thanks, Daddy. I think I'll go. I won't let mean ole Missy steal my joy, either!"

"That's my girl. Let's go downstairs and see who's at the door."

Kayla held Jake's hand tightly as they walked down the steps. Halfway down, he looked up and froze.

"Dr. Olivia!" Kayla yelled.

Jake blinked his eyes several times to make sure he wasn't seeing things. He wasn't imagining it. Olivia stood in his foyer wearing a dress exactly like the one hanging in Kayla's closet.

Kayla dropped his hand and raced to Olivia. "I knew you'd come. Daddy said you left, but I knew you'd come back."

Jake wasn't sure what to think. His first instinct was to protect his little girl. He couldn't bear the thought of her being hurt again.

Olivia opened her arms and picked Kayla off the ground. They twirled in a circle, both giggling.

When Olivia placed Kayla on her feet again, her eyes fixated on him.

His pulse raced.

"Hi, Jake." She smiled.

He cautiously moved toward her. His heart pounded in his chest. "What are you doing here?"

Olivia's eyes sparkled with tears. "If it's okay with you, I came to take Kayla to the fashion show."

"What about your job? Aren't you supposed to be there now?"

"I put in my notice this morning and got on the first flight to Denver. I just finished talking with Dr. Dickerson. He's going to start training me next week."

Myrna and Kyle cheered from the corner of the room.

Kyle raced to Jake's side. "Daddy, ask her now!"

Jake could hardly peel his eyes away from Olivia. He looked down at Kyle. "Ask what?"

"Ask Dr. Olivia on the date."

Jake reached for Olivia's hand. He planned to take Olivia on dates for the rest of their lives.

Epilogue

Fourteen months later

"Can I hold Maddie, Mommy?"

The word was sweet music to Olivia's ears. *Mommy.*

"I'll be careful. I promise," Kayla said.

Jake had spread out a blanket earlier for Olivia and their new daughter. He'd gone to grill hamburgers and hot dogs.

"Of course you can, sweetie. Have a seat."

Maddie cooed and squinted into the bright July sun reflecting off the lake. Olivia gave Maddie's sun bonnet a quick tug to protect her eyes.

A month had already passed since they welcomed Maddie into the family. Two days prior to her birth, Olivia had officially adopted Kayla and Kyle. Motherhood was exactly how she'd imagined. Exhausting, but so worth every lost hour of sleep.

"I love being a big sister." Kayla took Maddie and snuggled her in her arms.

"You're a wonderful big sister, and you're a tremendous help to me." Olivia leaned back and relaxed for the first time since the party had started.

Olivia couldn't believe she and Jake were already celebrating their anniversary at the same place they'd exchanged vows one year ago. Mirror Lake held a special place in her heart. It was where Jake brought her on their first date, and it was the spot Jake learned he was going to be a father again.

When he proposed, Jake wanted it to be a big surprise. He'd asked Olivia to come over to his house and watch the sunset on her favorite bench. She'd been back in Bluebell for three weeks and they'd been spending every non-working moment together. For the first time, she declined his invitation. She'd had a long day of training with Dr. Dickerson and was exhausted.

He showed up at Gammy's house with some story about a rare meteor shower that was happening. Olivia was intrigued and decided to go with him despite her tiredness. To this day, he told the story about how she almost missed her chance to become his wife.

"Hey, how come you get to take a break?" Jake stood over her, blocking the sun. She still couldn't believe this gorgeous man was her husband and the father of her child.

He flopped down onto the blanket next to Olivia. "I thought this was our anniversary party. Why am I stuck doing all the work?" Jake joked. "I thought that big rock on your finger meant we were a team."

Olivia laughed. One thing she loved most about Jake, besides the fact that he was a wonderful father, was his sense of humor. Laughter filled their days. "But you like to be in charge of the grill." She nudged her shoulder against his.

"Daddy, after you finish cooking for everyone, can you take me and Kyle out on the canoe?"

"Sure. I'll have to grab the life jackets from the truck. Where is Kyle?" Jake looked around.

"He and Miss Myrna took Callie for a walk."

Jake nodded and took Olivia's hand. "It's quite a turnout, huh?"

"Well, that's what happens when you put Gammy in charge of party invitations. The entire town shows up." Olivia wouldn't have it any other way. Their family and friends were a blessing.

"Hey, guys." Logan approached the blanket and removed his black Stetson. "I wanted to wish you both a happy anniversary. It's a fantastic party."

"Thanks, man. I appreciate it."

"Thank you, Logan," Olivia said.

Jake stood and addressed his brother. "We need to find you a nice girl so you can settle down."

Logan laughed. "No, thanks. I'm happy being single."

Olivia didn't believe Jake's brother. She'd have to work on that.

"Daddy, come quick!"

"That's Kyle!" Jake said and took off running.

Olivia took Maddie from Kayla's arms. "Let's go, Kayla."

"He's down by the lake," Jake called out over his shoulder. "He's okay. Gammy is with him."

Olivia, the baby and Kayla joined up with Jake. "What's going on?" Olivia looked down and saw Callie digging frantically in the sand. "What is she after?"

"I don't know. Gammy and I were walking, and Callie just started digging. I kept pulling her leash, but she wouldn't move," Kyle explained.

Jake knelt in the sand. "Would you look at this?" He reached his hand into the hole.

"It's your watch, Daddy! The one I lost!" Kyle yelled.

Olivia couldn't hold back her tears. She watched her husband and son celebrating the discovery of the lost family heirloom and thought *God is good*.

* * * * *

Dear Reader,

I hope you enjoyed reading Olivia and Jake's story. Like many of us, they faced difficult circumstances that made it difficult to trust God's plan for their lives.

As I continue to write, I face new challenges, especially during times of uncertainty when distractions can pull me off course. But I've learned I'm not alone on this journey. I'm grateful for the gift and desire to write stories of hope, and as long as I remain faithful to God's plan, I know He won't abandon me. Remembering this brings me peace, and I hope it does the same for you.

I invite you to join me in Bluebell Canyon for the next installment in the series, where you'll meet more lovely residents.

Hearing from readers is the best part of being a published author. I do my best to respond to every email. You can join my newsletter at jillweatherholt.com or drop me a note.

Blessings,
Jill Weatherholt